THE DEFENDER

#11

THE
CHALLENGE

Books by Jerry Ahern

The Survivalist Series

#1: Total War
#2: The Nightmare Begins
#3: The Quest
#4: The Doomsayer
#5: The Web
#6: The Savage Horde
#7: The Prophet
#8: The End is Coming
#9: Earth Fire
#10: The Awakening
#11: The Reprisal
#12: The Rebellion
#13: Pursuit
#14: The Terror

#15: Overlord
#16: The Arsenal
#17: The Ordeal
#18: The Struggle
#19: Final Rain
#20: Firestorm
#21: To End All War
#22: Brutal Conquest
#23: Call To Battle
#24: Blood Assassins
#25: War Mountain
#26: Countdown
#27: Death Watch
#28: Mid-Wake
#29: The Legend

The Defender Series

#1: The Battle Begins
#2: The Killing Wedge
#3: Out of Control
#4: Decision Time
#5: Entrapment
#6: Escape

#7: Vengeance
#8: Justice Denied
#9: Death Grip
#10: The Good Fight
#11: The Challenge
#12: No Survivors

They Call Me the Mercenary Series

#1: The Killer Genesis
#2: The Slaughter Run
#3: Fourth Reich Death Squad
#4: The Opium Hunter
#5: Canadian Killing Ground
#6: Vengeance Army
#7: Slave of the Warmonger
#8: Assassin's Express
#9: The Terror Contract

#10: Bush Warfare
#11: Death Lust!
#12: Headshot!
#13: Naked Blade, Naked Gun
#14: The Siberian Alternative
#15: The Afghanistan Penetration
#16: China Bloodhunt
#17: Buckingham Blowout
#18: Eye for Eye

THE DEFENDER

#11

THE
CHALLENGE

JERRY AHERN

SPEAKING VOLUMES, LLC

NAPLES, FLORIDA

2012

THE DEFENDER

#11 THE CHALLENGE

ISBN 978-1-61232-317-6

To the men and women who inspire us with their daily acts of heroism, however ordinary or magnificent, but never trivial . . .

Chapter One

SNOW BLEW COLD and wet, its tenuous hold to the rocks above him easy victim to the wind's relentless assault. The sheepskin collar of his coat, turned up against that same enemy, felt wet against his neck. It called to mind the haircut Lilly had given him, her laughter, her smile, the touch of her fingers against his skin. Now, his skin was numbing. And when he thought of Lilly and her warmth, somehow the cold was more intense. He set his jaw against that as he would against any other adversary and kept moving, the stiffness in his right knee working out gradually. Cold didn't affect it—a good thing under the circumstances—and neither did dampness—also a good thing. But the ride and keeping the knee in one basic position for three hours had.

When he'd learned to ride, his knee, like the rest of his body in those comparatively halcyon days of his youth, had been more or less perfect. Age sneaked up and perfection sneaked away, and sometimes he wondered if the cause of all of that were somehow a lack of vigilance. Because vigilance was something he had learned as well over the years since coming West, not something he'd been born with.

Araby whinnied.

"Quiet, horse," he muttered, clutching the H & K 91 rifle tighter in his fists. He continued to work his way downward.

When he reached the base of the V-shaped wedge of rock, he dropped to a low crouch and paused, holding his breath, listening for something other than the keening of the wind and the creaking of the pine boughs.

Only Araby whinnying again. He could have tied a bandana over her muzzle, but there were still a few wolves in these mountains and he didn't want to make it impossible for the animal to signal her distress to him, just in case. With the wind, and considering the distance, Araby would never be heard from the mesa across the canyon.

There was no other sound.

He dropped into a prone position, moving forward through the fresh snow on knees and elbows, the right knee feeling all but normal again as he advanced.

The spit of rock across which he crawled extended some fifty to sixty feet over the canyon floor below, a peninsula in the air. He was assaulted by the biting wind's full cyclonic effect even more than he had been when he'd ridden Araby up along the winding defile toward the summit. When the rocks and snow became impassable, he'd dismounted, eased the cinch on the three-quarter double-rigged stock saddle and dug into the saddlebags for the hobbles so she wouldn't spook and leave him stranded.

He was sentimental over Araby, not foolish.

At last he reached the farthest edge of the rock. Before he set down his rifle, he checked in all four directions.

He was alone here and that was what he wanted.

He put the rifle down in the snow, careful to keep the muzzle clear of it. He reached to the binocular case, opened it, took out the armored eight-by-thirties, and brought them to his eyes. It was harder to manipulate the center focus ring with gloved fingers, but he wasn't in a hurry.

Below him was the river, wildly churning white water and rocks that logic dictated should have been worn smooth generations ago. He'd run that river. Logic be damned in its case.

On the far side of the canyon, on an islandlike mesa, lay the complex. He thought of it as a "complex" for lack of a more all-encompassing term. The aggregate of interconnected blockhouses surrounding the multistoried central structure was at once a compound—it was surrounded with high concrete-block walls crowned with barbed wire —and a bastion. Its presence commanded the canyon on all sides and the river running through the canyon and the solitary natural access from the far side of the mountain. Into the mountain's face had been cut a two-lane road, and a solitary set of railroad tracks was laid knifing upward, terminating within those walls. It was the fastest construction job he'd ever seen, all prefabricated units but assembled of solid materials, to last.

The train Lilly's son, Wisdom, had seen had nearly chugged to the walls themselves now.

He set down the glasses, pulled the brim of his Stetson lower over his face, and tightened the knot in the woolen scarf bound over it, the scarf covering his ears and tied under his chin, warming him and preventing his hat from blowing off.

A cigar would be good right now.

And there was little likelihood anyone would see the smoke.

Little likelihood was too much of a gamble, so he decided to forgo it.

He hugged the H & K rifle to him, blowing away some of the snow the wind wasn't taking care of, keeping the weapon as dry as he could. He owned exactly two rifles, one shotgun, and three handguns, plus a wealth of replacement parts for each, all the weapons carefully chosen, all the best, accessorized as necessary to make them better. And all of his weapons were scrupulously maintained.

Only three firearms were with him now, the 7.62mm H & K rifle, the Beretta 92F 9mm Parabellum on his hip, and the Beretta 950 BS .25 caliber automatic that was his hideout gun. He'd gotten used to that concept—the hideout gun—during his days in law enforcement.

The solitary shotgun, a Remington 870 pump, along with the .54 caliber T/C Hawken rifle and the Ruger Old Army percussion .44, were with Lilly. The shotgun was for occasional use only, when a shotgun and nothing else would do, which usually translated to taking Wisdom hunting. The two cap-and-ball arms, both the rifle and the revolver, were kept in the event that prefabricated ammunition and/or reloading components to manufacture metallic cartridges became totally unavailable. He could cast his own lead balls, round or conical, make his own black powder, and fabricate his own percussion caps.

He detested the smell of molten lead, however, and liked the convenience and efficiency of commercial ammunition or hand-loaded ammunition from commercially manufactured components. He was in no immediate danger of running out of either, having stocked up over the last several years as the tide of sentiment against trusting free men to own firearms as was their constitutional right had devolved to frenzied hysteria.

The train, armed snow-smocked guards on the roofs of boxcars and moving about on the flatcars, was about to enter the compound. He set down his rifle and picked up his binoculars. He didn't envy those men. The cold they had to have endured on the long ride up the mountain must have been unbearable.

The massive steel outer gates of the compound wall were opening, the engine passing beside the deflection barriers, which could be raised or lowered to block entrance to vehicles. The deflection barriers were positioned so that even if an enemy vehicle were to approach in the wrong lane, it could be just as easily stopped.

The engine, a quite modern-looking diesel, pulled four boxcars that were sealed, three passenger cars, a baggage car, several tank cars, and a half dozen flatcars, these located four at the center and one immediately behind the engine, the last one immediately before the caboose. These two flatcars separated from the rest were fitted with antiaircraft emplacements protected by sandbagged machine-gun nests. The remaining four flatcars carried additional building materials for the completion of the complex.

He exhaled a long breath, the steam dissipating before the objective lenses of the binoculars. It would be a long morning. . . .

Elmer Fulton's description of the trucks and the general direction in which they had moved after leaving the Metro railroad yard had, after considerable effort over a period of six days, led them here, to this.

The sound of steel scraping dirt as shovels were worked, the wind in the trees, the murmurs of the men digging, and the persons standing around what no one wanted to say would prove to be, but everyone feared was a mass grave.

David Holden clambered up out of the hole, passed his spade over to Tommy Kellogg for a turn, and dusted off his gloved hands as he went to stand beside Rosie Shepherd. Luther Steel passed him, shovel in hand, face downturned and grim, on his way to dig some more.

Young Barnabas Wood, the Army lieutenant because of whose escape the Patriots had first learned that military officers and ranking noncoms were the prisoners of the Presidential Strike Force, stood unsteadily beside Rosie. It had proven impossible to prevent Wood from taking up a shovel, so they'd helped him into the hole, given him a shovel, and let him dig until he was too weak to continue. The gunshot wound Wood had sustained in his leg during the first moments of his escape had become infected and his fever had only broken forty-eight hours ago. But Holden gave the young man with the oddly long nose credit for guts.

As Holden approached, Rosie lit a cigarette, exhaled, and passed it to Holden. "Thanks." He nodded, turning around, staring back at the hole. The sun was nearly to its zenith for this bleak autumn day, and the wind that blew across the clearing in the mountain woods was cold and unremitting in its velocity. Holden burrowed his shoulders deeper into his coat against it as he exhaled the smoke.

"How deep are you?" Rosie asked him softly.

"About eight feet. Nothing yet. But those kids said they saw men in military uniforms digging here."

"Why aren't you letting me help?"

"Women don't get to use shovels; shovels are too technologically sophisticated," Holden told her, forcing a smile he didn't feel. The quiet, the somber expressions, all were funereal, and with just cause, Holden thought.

"Bullshit," Rosie commented after a second, then moved over to stand closer to him. . . .

The train was beginning to disgorge its occupants, at least three dozen men in white snow smocks, black M-16 rifles slung across their backs, these men in addition to the ones still positioned atop the boxcar roofs and on the flatcars. They were likely more of the Presidential Strike Force rather than regular Army personnel, he thought, momentarily moving the binoculars from his eyes, squinting, then looking through the binoculars again.

The men from inside the train were forming up in ranks, a man in camouflage fatigues, with what appeared to be a pistol holster on each side of his belt, swinging down from the lead passenger car to walk about officiously in the snow.

It would have been interesting to overhear what might be said to these troops, but with the observation equipment available—nothing more than binoculars—such was impossible.

He rested his eyes again, watching the motion of the river far below him, shook his head, returned to the binoculars.

The troops were formed. Two-holsters was obviously addressing them. "Probably telling them what a pompous asshole you are, hmm?' No, well, you should be!"

After what seemed longer subjectively, but he realized was only about two minutes, the formation was dismissed and some of the men who had been part of it climbed up onto the boxcar roofs or moved onto the flatcars to relieve the guards stationed there. The rest positioned themselves near the boxcar doors in semicircles, M-16's held at the hip for close-range firing. At a gesture (presumably accompanied by a verbal command from Two-holsters, who stood well away from the boxcars, separated from the cars by the semicircle formation), men rushed forward at the double to begin opening the boxcar doors.

The doors of all four boxcars were opened almost synchronously, the Presidential Strike Force personnel rushing back.

An order was apparently given, and slowly, ragged-looking men began to appear in the boxcar doors, some of them jumping down into the snow, others seeming to fall. From one of the boxcars women of equally disheveled appearance emerged. None of the personnel offloading from the box-cars seemed dressed for the cold weather.

The PSF guards moved in, prodding the personnel from the boxcars into a ragged formation.

One woman fell to her knees and didn't get up. A guard prodding her along rifle-butted her in the head. One of the male prisoners tried to jump the guard. Rifle shots—full auto—crackled across the frigid morning air.

He put down his binoculars, rolling onto his back as he pulled his hat off, his right fist, beside the butt of his pistol, opening and closing impotently.

He ran his gloved fingers back through his hair.

He heard Araby whinnying softly.

He made the sign of the cross. . . .

At a little over nine feet deep David Holden and Luther Steel, standing back to back in the hole, which had broadened into a pit, simultaneously hit an object with their shovels that felt harder than earth and softer than a rock.

They scraped away more dirt with their shovels for several seconds.

And then there was a terrible smell of rotting flesh.

Chapter Two

THE SNOW WAS forming in his mustache as he breathed, and the condensation was refreezing.

He pulled his hat lower over his eyes against the blowing snow. His ears were cold, but after he'd pulled off his hat there on the peninsula of rock above the canyon, throwing the black Stetson down into the snow, he hadn't bothered with the woolen scarf again. He wasn't about to bother with it, either, until he was back on Araby and riding away from here.

Although a patriot, he wasn't a Patriot. He'd given up a long time ago on joining things that involved masses of people. The Kalispell Patriot Cell leader and Lilly's older brother, Bob Twobears, had asked him to go up into the high lonesomes because, as he'd put it, "You know that country better than any Indian alive, and you're white. We need to know what's going on at that base the PSF's built up there." Bob Twobears had added that Lilly would want him to go but, of course, would never ask him to risk his life.

As he waded through the drifted snow in the rocky V-notch and toward Araby, the wind was blowing the snow so hard, he could barely see the half-Arabian chestnut mare. He couldn't stop thinking about Lilly's brother and he muttered under his breath, "Well, you know now, Twobears. Now you know. It's a death camp."

He tugged off his right glove, then his left, so he could work the Zippo lighter properly and fire his cigar.

"Hold it! Right where you are!"

At the first sound of the voice his shoulders had hunched up and his right arm had begun to move. The H & K rifle, slung over his shoulder, was too slow to get to, but he'd started to reach for the 9mm in the flap holster at his hip.

A burst of assault-rifle fire drilled into the rock wall of the V-notch and he knew there wasn't the chance; so he didn't move anymore.

He looked up. Two men with white snow-smocks partially covering woodland camouflage battle dress utilities were aiming M-16's at him from waist level. Both men stood in the high rocks beside which he'd tethered Araby, taking advantage of the rocks as a windbreak for her.

"Up with your hands!"

He looked at the two men with disgust, feeling an equal if differently motivated disgust for himself at having walked into the trap they'd set. On the plus side, he at last had confirmation that small PSF patrol units were moving about on this side of the river.

He raised his hands.

"You're in deep shit, fella."

"Is that a fact?"

"That's a rifle on your shoulder and a handgun on your hip," the one who'd spoken before shouted down to him.

"You, sir, are very observant."

"Shut the fuck up and keep those hands high!"

He shrugged his shoulders slightly, eyeing Araby. She seemed unmolested, and with men such as these the literal meaning of the word wasn't too much of a stretch for the imagination.

It was important that they come down close to him, at least one of them; and almost as if they read his desires but not the motivation behind them, the one who hadn't spoken started down out of the rocks, while the one who'd spoken stayed where he was, the M-16's muzzle unwavering.

Options were limited, not unpromising.

Patiently, his gloveless hands quite cold, he waited.

At last, after more than a minute, the silent PSF man was on the ground and starting toward him. His silence broke. "Don't you even fuckin' twitch."

Evidently, a limited vocabulary was a determining qualification for membership in the Presidential Strike Force.

"I rarely twitch."

"Shut up!"

He shrugged his shoulders slightly.

The man stopped about six feet away. "Nice and easy, I want you to shrug outa that sling and let that rifle fall."

The scope and mounts were in his saddlebags anyway, and the snow was soft.

He lowered his right arm and shoulder and let the H & K rifle fall away, then smiled at the man.

"Good boy. Now, raise that right hand and with your left hand unbuckle that gun belt."

"If you say so." He nodded.

Slowly, he moved his left arm down and bent slightly to undo the thong that held the holster semirigidly to his calf. As he bent, he also shifted body position slightly so the man in front of him was between him and the one still some distance away up in the rocks.

The holster and belt were prized possessions, a "1940 Outfit" handcrafted of black leather by El Paso Saddlery, consisting of a 1911 belt with solid brass two-piece "U.S."

buckle, a 1940 full-flap holster suspended below a 1911 drop-shank belt hanger, a 1911 double-magazine pouch.

His left hand moved to the buckle, undoing it.

"No funny stuff."

"I assure you; nothing I do will amuse you." He let the holster and the military Beretta inside it fall to the snow, his left hand moving easily to his trouser belt, beneath his sweater. He dodged left, the first two fingers of his fist closing around the butt of the .25, his left thumb sweeping down the frame-mounted safety, over to the hammer and jacking it back to full cock as the man six feet away from him moved the assault rifle's muzzle to intercept the plane of his body.

Not fast enough.

He fired the .25 three times, once to the solar plexus, once to the chest, and once to the thorax as the already dying man's assault rifle sprayed uselessly into the snow.

A burst of assault-rifle fire came also from the rocks above, where the second man stood; but it hit the first man. No time to worry, just time to act, he rolled left into the snow, dropping the .25 because the range was too great for the forty-grain hardball's terminal energy and he had more important things to do with his left hand. His right hand tore open the flap of the El Paso holster, his left hand wrenching the holster away, his right hand closing around the 9mm's butt.

He stabbed the 9mm upward toward the man shooting at him.

Something—a bullet, logically—tore at his left upper arm and his first two shots went wild as he was thrown off balance. He rolled through the snow a full 360 degrees, his hat lost, the snow near him churning under the multiple impacts of rifle bullets. He punched the 92F forward again, this time almost to the full extension of his right arm. He fired a double tap, then another.

The PSF trooper firing at him with the M-16 ceased all visible motion, stood stock still. Then, almost imperceptibly at first, the man's body began to sway, then fall.

It skidded down across the rocks, head down into a snowdrift.

He stood up with the Beretta 9mm Parabellum pistol still in his right fist.

The first order of business was to check the men, although he was certain they were dead. Araby was making a commotion and he looked at her. The shots, experienced though she was to gunfire,—had nonetheless frightened her. "Easy, Araby."

He checked the one he'd shot three times with the little .25 auto. Eyes wide open, no pulse. He nodded his head, his right knee bothering him a little as he went to the second man. Also dead.

He looked at the gun in his hand, nodded his head, worked the safety down to drop the hammer, and shoved the pistol into his belt.

It was open war now.

There was a considerable amount to do in very little time. It would have been foolish self-delusion to believe he was out of the woods. His left upper arm was bleeding—he didn't think badly, but bleeding nonetheless. If two PSF men were on this side of the river, there had to be a minimum of eight or a dozen more, and the gunfire would bring them here, perhaps with all-terrain vehicles that could easily outrun Araby. He considered the M-16 rifles briefly, but decided against subjecting Araby to the unnecessary weight.

He decocked the Beretta, flicking the safety off, sliding the pistol into his belt.

He bent to the man half buried in the snow, reached to the pistol belt there, and removed the two spare Beretta magazines from it, then the man's pistol, taking the magazine from it as well. The ammunition might prove useful, although he had no need for additional magazines. He did the same with the first dead PSF trooper, then moved on quickly.

He found his hat, shook snow from it, cocked it on the back of his head.

The Beretta .25. It would need a cleaning, of course, but seemed undamaged. His left arm was stiffening, so he didn't attempt to lower the hammer, a two-handed operation, merely upping the diminutive pistol's safety, pocketing it rather than replacing it inside the waistband of his trousers.

His gun belt. He slung that over his shoulder, then walked over to his rifle.

The rifle was half covered with blowing snow, but seemed otherwise unaffected.

He caught it up and started toward Araby, thrusting the rifle into the rearward-facing saddle boot on the right side of the saddle.

He took a moment, stroking her neck to calm the wide-eyed look in her eyes. "Proof that animals must be smarter than people, hmm?" And he looked first at one, then the other of the two dead men. . . .

His gas mask on to protect himself from the smell, David Holden's gloved hands reached into the center of the pit. He found a grip on one of the dead bodies—a female officer with rotting gray skin and a large blackened bullet hole in her left cheek—and pulled, Steel helping him. As he started to swing the body up to the waiting Patriots at the lip of the grave, he realized he was handing the dead woman to Rosie.

Holden's and Rosie's eyes met.

He merely nodded, saying nothing about her handling the bodies, then continued with his work.

Chapter Three

THE STAMINA OF the Arabian showed in her now, as it always seemed to when he needed it most. Skidding on her haunches, she took him almost effortlessly down the defile and toward the woods.

His left arm was numbing and stiff at his side and he was cold, but the bleeding, as far as he was able to discern, was stanched. She moved as if sensing the urgency with which they rode, because the stray hare that would dart across their path or the owl hooting in the trees—occurrences that usually elicited at least a toss of her great head—were totally ignored in her single-minded headlong lunge.

He'd bought Araby as a yearling and raised her himself. Her deep chestnut coloring, the black mane and tail, the broad forehead of the Arab, and her obvious size for a mare, had appealed to him from the moment he'd first set eyes on her. As a boy he'd ridden horses on his uncle's Iowa farm. And that was where he'd learned to hunt and fish as well. Adulthood flung him at times from one corner of the earth to the other, but hunting, fishing, and horses were always his means of temporary escape to sanity.

Twelve years ago he had given up his badge and made the escape permanent.

Three years ago he had bought Araby, the finest animal he'd ever ridden. She was bright, she was loyal, she was constant, she was beautiful, she was willing. If she'd been a human female, he could almost have married her—except for Lilly Twobears. Theirs was an "understanding" of proportions he'd never contemplated.

"Whoa, whoa, Araby," he called, and Araby, flinging her head back, pulled up short, feet planted, unmoving, waiting.

He leaned down in the saddle, his eyes scanning the snow ahead for any sign of the Presidential Strike Force's presence, at the same time slipping his right foot out of the stirrup and flexing his knee. "It appears we're alone, but let's go slowly just in case," he told her, urging her ahead gently as he put his right foot back into the stirrup, but holding well back on her reins so she wouldn't bolt into the woods.

She loved running and would have run herself into the ground if he let her.

He put her reins in his teeth for a moment, pulled his collar up and his hat down, and tugged at the knotted woolen scarf under his chin. At a normal pace in this weather the ride between the overlook and where he'd camped the night would consume approximately three hours, and it was another seven hours at a similar pace to Trapper Springs, where Lilly would have warm soup in the kettle and a warm bath for him to soak in and a glass of good whiskey to warm his insides—and that smile that he could see sometimes when he closed his eyes.

Mechanically, he checked his gear, then shifted the reins back to his right hand. "Easy, Araby," he cautioned. He was going to ride her straight through with a few brief stops and calculated that with one hour behind him and about six hours more, he and Araby could both rest. . . .

* * *

From the obvious appearance of some of the wounds to the already partially decomposing bodies, it was evident that nonmilitary weapons had been used. Selecting bodies that looked the easiest to work with, and after realizing there was nothing more left inside him to vomit up, with the help of Bill Runningdeer, Holden began to dig for projectiles.

Runningdeer, who had been a biology major before switching from science to accounting and law enforcement, was handy with a knife and, thank God, neat and economical as he cut. Runningdeer too, however, early on, lost his breakfast.

Under a tarp and well away from the rest of the men and women assembled in and around the field, some still digging for more bodies, Holden and Runningdeer did their grisly work until a sufficient number of projectiles had been recovered.

Then the task of identifying the projectiles fell to Steel and Rosie.

Convinced that, even if they had not done enough, they could stomach no more, Holden and Runningdeer ceased their work by late afternoon. More bodies had been found in a second grave, the count well over sixty now, and new holes were being dug.

Rosie and Luther Steel worked off the back of a pickup truck at the far end of the clearing. Clouds, more threatening than before, loomed over the mountains to the west. Burrowing his hands into his pockets, Holden crossed the clearing to join them at the pickup, where a windbreak had been set up.

They wore rubber gloves, as Holden and Runningdeer had. There were small piles of projectiles set out and magnifying glasses and live rounds of every description, both assembled and disassembled.

Holden stepped up between them, Rosie saying to him without looking at him, "I'm glad you and Bill stopped. We have enough anyway."

"You think *you're* glad." When he closed his eyes, Holden could still see the human remains with which he and Runningdeer had worked and he thought he might see them in his dreams.

"These are thirty-eight Specials over here," Steel began. "Thirty-eights and three fifty-sevens. About all we can do is match approximate mass and shape and make an educated guess."

"That's all that's required at this point." Holden nodded.

"All right, then," Rosie said, gesturing to the pile of projectiles nearest her. "These are thirty-caliber pellets like you'd find in twelve-gauge double-0 buck loads. And these are twenty-two round-nosed lead. They're about the same size—they'd be lighter—as the ones in this smaller pile, twenty-fives. The twenty-fives retained most of their gilding metal jackets. These are various nine-millimeter-sized bullets, either from legitimate nine-millimeter Parabellum rounds or three eighties, but you'll notice that next to the twenty-fives, that's the smallest pile. Then we have some forty-five ACPs. But all of these," and she pointed to the largest pile in the middle, "are thirty-odd-thirties, seven-millimeters, forty-fours, and a lot more thirty-eight and three fifty-seven. With the exception of the nine millimeters and the forty-fives, there's not a round that was used that could possibly be military. Some military units still have thirty-eight Special Model Fifteen Smiths, but that's increasingly rarer these days. What it all means is that they executed these poor people with weapons that the government confiscated from the civilian population. And you know why."

David Holden looked away from the truck bed and studied the toes of his combat boots. His boots were covered with dirt from the gravesites. "To make anybody seeing this think we did it. Damn them."

Chapter Four

CROSSING THE VALLEY would have been quicker, but it would be easier for the PSF to spot them as well, so he guided Araby north in a wide circle around its perimeter, staying to the high ground. Blood was smeared over the face of his wristwatch as he tried to raise his left arm with his right hand. Six hours had gone by, at least one more remaining until Trapper Springs, if Araby could do without another rest.

And he hoped that she could. If he dismounted, he realized he might never be able to get back up again.

He could barely stay upright in the saddle, but forced himself to while he took the rope from the latigo carrier on the right side of the fork, Araby's reins in his teeth again. His left arm alternately ached like an infected tooth or felt totally absent from his body.

"Desperate times require desperate measures, Araby."

He shook out a wide loop and—awkwardly because he could only use one hand, whispering to Araby more as he did—flipped the loop over himself, locking the burner with a hitch on the inside so the loop wouldn't close, then securing the leading end to the horn of his saddle, dropping the coiled remainder over the horn.

Tied to the saddle now as securely as he could make it with one hand, he whispered to Araby, telling her, "Take me to Lilly, girl. Take me to Lilly." Araby was smart, could find her way home to her stall; but she wouldn't be wary for the PSF. Still, she was his only chance now.

He slumped forward a little in the saddle and, without wanting to, closed his eyes. . . .

Geoffrey Kearney came up out of the water and pushed his hair back from his eyes. He shivered slightly, but the ocean was warmer than the water in the pool and he'd needed the solitude. The burnout from being turned on twenty-four hours a day was the greatest danger to the agent working in deep cover.

But at least he recognized its signs and compensated as best he could. He was beginning to worry about Linda.

Six days of pretending to be a person she was not and never could be—although she was carrying it off well—was taking its toll.

"Thad! Over here!"

Kearney responded to the name of his current persona and waved back to Dimitri Borsoi, in slacks and a heavy sweater, his still-bad legs propped up on the foot of a long, folding lounger beside the pool. Thad Borden, Geoffrey Kearney's current alter ego, was a difficult identity to maintain but an easy one to step away from, because Thad was an immoral street punk who'd never grown up, never had much schooling, and thrived on his own villainy.

Kearney grabbed up his towel, sweatshirt, and sweatpants from the sand and jogged up toward the rear of the house. This beach house, about ten miles from the one where Kearney had first met Borsoi, was vastly larger, vastly better appointed, and vastly more secure.

At any of numerous times in the past six days, he could have killed Dimitri Borsoi with relative ease. He had free access not only to his own weapons but to the considerable supply of weapons stored within the house. Two things, however, had prevented him from exercising that option. One was that he wasn't yet certain about Borsoi's place in the FLNA scheme of things, nor for that matter how tight was the connection between the FLNA and the man in the Oval Office, Roman Makowski. Did the FLNA wholly manipulate Makowski, or was Makowski merely an ally? The second mitigating factor was that, once he killed Borsoi, he'd be faced with getting out of Borsoi's beachfront compound alive, along with Linda Effingham, in the face of considerable heavily armed opposition.

For the time being, Dimitri Borsoi—or Mr. Johnson, as Borsoi liked being called by his imbecilic pimply-faced American gang-banger stooges—was as safe as church.

As Kearney slowed for the steps leading up the side of the embankment to the level of the house, he saw Linda. She was playing the part to the hilt, spending most of the day getting along with Borsoi's roommate Vanessa and the other women of the household—which meant drinking a little too much, smoking a little too much, swearing a little too much, and generally behaving as though, in the middle of the night, someone had sneaked up beside her and sucked out her brains with a very efficient vacuum cleaner.

As Kearney reached the level of the pool deck, pulling the sweatshirt over him, Borsoi—in a jovial mood all day—told him, "Make yourself a drink Thad."

"Makes my head buzzy I drink this early, Mr. Johnson."

Borsoi smiled genuinely. "Suit yourself. Sit down. I want to talk with you."

"You bet," Kearney agreed, crossing around the pool and pulling up a chair. He dusted the sand off his feet and stepped into his sweatpants—it was cold here with the wind blowing—and stood up to pull them on then sat down again. "What can I do you for?" Kearney smiled.

"I've been enjoying your company, Thad. Maybe it's

that you're older than most of the rest of them and speak well enough that English is still recognizable as your native language—I'm not sure."

"Whatchya mean?"

"I'm not sure about you. Why are you here?"

Kearney's palms began to sweat a little and he wished he had his cigarettes and lighter—or a gun. "Ya asked me, Mr. Johnson."

Borsoi smiled indulgently. "I know that, Thad. But, a man like you, why aren't you doing something with your life?"

The answers to that were blocked out neatly in the identity established for him by his people in London and their people in Canada. "Well, man, ya know, uhh—after I got out—"

"What exactly were you in prison for?"

By now, of course, Borsoi had run every check possible on Thad Borden and knew all the answers. So, this was some sort of test. "Killed some son of a bitch. All I was doin' was movin' this shit—"

"Drugs?"

"Yeah."

"What kind?"

Kearney laughed. "Coke. If I'd hung out a little longer, hell, crack's easier to hide," and he laughed again.

"Why did you kill the man?"

"He was, kinda, interferin'. He was heeled anyways."

"So, you shot him?"

"Yeah."

"How did you feel afterward?"

"I got caught, Mr. Johnson." Kearney laughed. "I didn't feel so good, ya know?"

All humor was gone from Borsoi's face. "I meant, how did you feel about the killing?"

He didn't quite know what he was supposed to answer, so he said essentially that. "What am I supposed to say?"

"Did it bother you?"

Kearney shrugged. "Bothered me I got tossed in the slammer. That's about it."

Borsoi was apparently satisfied. He sipped at his drink. The girls—Linda among them—could be heard laughing from just inside, beyond the sliding doors. "I've never seen anyone slicker than you were that night at the party, the way you disarmed Harv. Where'd you learn that?"

" 'Nam."

"What did you do in Vietnam?"

Kearney put his hands together, flexed the fingers in and out, and looked down at them. "Long-range recon stuff."

"So, you went behind enemy lines and killed people. How many?"

"What? I don't—"

"Confirmed. How many?"

"Fifty-two."

"How?"

"I don't—"

"How?"

"Shoot 'em, slit their fuckin' throats, shit like that. Who keeps score?"

"Do you have an inkling of why I live here, why I have weapons and the authorities don't attempt to molest me, why I have unlimited money—and unlimited power?"

Kearney looked away at the wind-rippled surface of the pool, then back at Borsoi. "Figured you was into drugs, ya know?"

"Some of my financing comes from drugs. But that's not what I'm into, as you put it."

"Then . . ." Kearney let it hang.

"I'm very well connected in the Front for the Liberation of North America."

"They're commies, ain't they?"

Borsoi laughed. "Does that really matter when I'm offering you a chance at more wealth and power than you ever dreamed of?"

Geoffrey Kearney sometimes found himself wishing that violent megalomaniacs would form a union or something and find themselves better writers.

Give or take a bit of phrasing and ethnic color, it was likely the same speech used at one time or another by Adolf Hitler, Joseph Stalin, or the Ayatollah Khomeini.

Chapter Five

SHE WAS REREADING *Atlas Shrugged*, Ayn Rand's words truer by the day.

Lilly Twobears set the book down on top of the afghan covering her legs, lifted afghan and book and set them on the footstool—she never used it—and stood up, the hem of her skirt falling almost to her ankles.

The clock on the mantle below Matthew's Hawken rifle showed that it was well past time for starting dinner. But with Wisdom away at her sister's house for a week and Matthew off on her brother's business, cooking wasn't any fun. So time didn't matter. She crossed the cabin's great room, took the three steps up into the kitchen, found the bottle of port, and poured a glass, more than half the bottle still left.

She sipped at the wine and it warmed her instantly as, mentally, she pursued its course through her body.

As a girl, growing up on the reservation and watching men—her brother never among them—going off and blasting their minds with alcohol and enforcing poverty on their women and children, she had read *Atlas* for the first time and told herself that, when she was grown, she would find "John Galt" and marry him. As she'd gotten older, the book and everything it stood for had ceased to have meaning for her until she met Matthew Smith. Her own marriage had dissolved and then, just when she'd screwed up the courage to do what was unthinkable for her tribe and get a divorce, the man she'd married—no relation but the same last name—had died.

It was the same year Matthew Smith quit the United States Marshals Service and came west to Montana.

The first time she'd seen him, not knowing him, she'd been unable to understand the contradictory elements of his nature, and the more she learned of him, the more confused, for a time, she became.

He was often dour faced, yet he had a wonderful laugh that lit his eyes and totally consumed him. He was tough, yet he was incredibly patient and could be quite gentle and his speech was dignified; yet his anger, when sufficiently aroused, was terrible beyond anything she had ever seen, although never misdirected.

He rode a horse well, something that endeared him at once to Wisdom, who had ridden before he could walk.

He dressed habitually in dark clothing, and when he wore a handgun on his hip—as he had done increasingly since the government had begun to fall apart—with his Stetson and his boots he looked like the gunslinger in some silly white man's movie about the western frontier of more than a century ago.

For years she had despaired of finding a man to love who was someone she could unflinchingly admire. She had wondered if such men existed outside of books.

Matthew Smith was unique, an individual whose only standards of conduct rose from within himself. He was his own yardstick, his own measure.

She fell hopelessly in love with him. That was seven years after Matthew Smith had come to Montana. For the last five they'd had their "understanding." Her mother hated him, because it was much better to be married to a drunk—her mother had remarried, picking a man almost identical to Lilly's father—than "live in sin" with a man who was fine and decent and true.

Lilly Twobears took another sip of port from her wineglass, threw her long hair back from her shoulders, and walked slowly across the room toward the easy chair by the fire.

She never sat in Matthew Smith's chair when he was at home, but she sat in it always when he was away. The subtle smell of his cigars—he smoked few of them and they were good cigars—and just the contours of the chair reminded her of him in a way so sensual that sometimes she would get up and leave the chair because, if she stayed in it, she would have cried.

She walked past the chair and got two small pieces from the woodpile Matthew had stacked for her before leaving, setting them carefully into the hearth.

The idea with a fire, Matthew had told her, as if, growing up an Indian woman, she had never known that for herself, was to nurse it, not allow it to gorge itself.

Wisdom's picture from school. She studied it there on the mantel. He looked so terribly/wonderfully white. His good shirt, one of the ties Matthew so rarely wore but looked so good wearing, his hair combed just right, his dark eyes defiant but gentle.

When they had moved permanently up to the cabin, school was gone forever—or, at least, until these troubles ended.

She would miss the pictures of Wisdom most of all.

"Wisdom Twobears," she said aloud. It was a fine name.

She took the second picture from the mantle and studied this more carefully. Her brother, Bob, the professional Indian and now the Patriot leader, had taken it a year ago.

There she was, in a skirt and just a heavy shawl, playing

in the snow like some silly child, in a snowball fight with Wisdom and with Matthew.

She lost the battle, but had so much fun doing it, she smiled now at the memory.

She studied Matthew Smith's face in the photograph.

It was a strong face. Although she found it handsome, some might not. His face bespoke his character.

She smiled, replacing the framed photograph on the mantle over the fire.

Above the mantle Matthew's Hawken rifle hung.

She went back to the chair, sat down, pulling her feet up under her skirt and arranging the afghan around her legs. There would be plenty of time for dinner, just something light. She picked up her book.

But as she took a sip from her glass, she heard something in the snow outside the house and almost spilled the wine.

Lilly Twobears sat bolt upright, drawing her legs up tighter. She heard the noise again. It was a horse in trouble. And then she heard the barking of dogs.

She was up, the glass of wine going onto the little end table beside the chair, cocooning the afghan around her shoulders. She needed boots and a gun. Her warm boots were by the door, but Matthew's shotgun was closer.

She crossed the room to the kitchen, reached into the broom cabinet, and took out the gun. Although the magazine held more, he kept the gun with only five rounds loaded and the chamber empty. Lashed to the wooden buttstock was a leather shell carrier that looked like the upper from a man's boot, five more rounds in it.

She ran to the door, the afghan half falling from her shoulders, but catching it up.

Pushing a curtain back as she heard the panicked whinnying again, she looked into the yard. About a hundred feet from the house Araby was on her hind legs, defending herself against three—no, four—feral dogs, each of them the size of a German shepherd, coming at her to snap at her legs. And, slumped over the saddle, as if he could barely hold on— "Matthew!"

She inverted her boots, shook them, pushed her feet into them. With frozen feet she'd be no good to Matthew or anyone. There wasn't time to lace the boots, knee-high moccasin style. She tore at the lock on the front door, threw the door open, racking the shotgun as she ran. The range was too great, but she fired the shotgun any-way. . . .

His left hand wouldn't respond and his right hand couldn't undo the knot; and it was a good rope, so he didn't want to cut it. "Damn," he hissed under his breath. Araby reared again. While he was lashed to her saddle, he couldn't get a steady shot at the feral dogs, and if Araby fell, she'd break his back.

He was starting to open the flap on the 1940 holster anyway, but he heard the report of a shotgun and sent a glance toward the cabin door. "Get back inside, Lilly!" But she was running through the snow toward them anyway and the dogs hadn't pulled off. They'd been shot at before, he realized, or were terribly hungry, because the snows had come very early this year.

He bit off the glove on his right hand, then reached to the side pocket of his coat for the folding knife there. A fixed-blade knife was in his saddlebags, but he'd never reach it in time. Even though his hand was cold, he got the knife—a black Fazendeiro—open with one hand, pinching the blade out and flipping down its butt end with his thumb. He raked it across the length of rope between the loop around his midsection and the horn of his saddle, severing it, flipping the knife away and trying to eyeball where it landed as he rolled out of the saddle when Araby reared again.

He fell into the deep snow, the wind knocked out of him. As he'd known they would, the dog pack turned its attention from Araby and came right at him.

His head was facing away from them and he rolled onto his back, his left arm coming alive with pain, but his right hand tearing open the flap on the El Paso holster. He pulled the Beretta from the leather, wiping off the safety as he made the draw.

The nearest of the dogs—some kind of unappealing-looking cross between a German shepherd and some other of the larger breeds—lunged for his throat.

He fired, a single shot, then a double tap into the animal's mouth, the dog's body whipping back and away, falling dead inches from his right foot.

Two more of the dogs were coming at him.

He fired, killing one of them with a double tap into the lungs. The second one was coming too fast. He rolled, the dog impacting the snow inches from him. As he brought the pistol up, he heard Lilly's voice. "Smith! Duck!"

He burrowed into the snow.

She wasn't all that good with a shotgun, but there wasn't time to argue.

He heard the shotgun discharge, heard a yelp, heard the racking of the pump.

And he heard Araby.

He looked up, stabbing the Beretta outward as the last of the four dogs—bigger than all the rest of them, it seemed—threw itself for Araby's throat.

As he fired, he heard the blast of the shotgun again. As his own bullet connected—he couldn't risk a double tap because Araby might be struck—he heard more yelping from the dog behind him. The dog going for Araby's throat seemed to pause in midair, then dropped.

He crawled through the snow for a foot or two, pulled himself up on his knees, standing shakily.

The dog behind him had been struck twice with the shotgun, but pellet imprints were all over the snow around it, more luck than skill on Lilly's part that the feral dog was dead and he wasn't.

He whistled to Araby and she pranced toward him. He safed the Beretta and thrust it into his holster. "Easy, baby."

"Smith!"

He turned away from his horse, Lilly coming into his arm. "Easy, baby," he told her.

Chapter Six

LEM PERRISH STOOD on the roof of the Marbletop Building, Metro's first real skyscraper, dwarfed by the more modern buildings surrounding it but still affording a clear view of the downtown area.

He was, somehow, reminded of the journalist in Orson Welles's 1938 Mercury Theater production of *War of the Worlds,* the man standing atop the office building and looking out into New Jersey as the clouds of gas from the Martian machines advanced inexorably upon New York City.

There was nothing extraterrestrial here, and gas—although it had been used periodically in the last few days to dispel rioters—was not in evidence now. The machines were tanks, and the creatures who piloted them, like the creatures huddled around them, were men, the Presidential Strike Force.

"I got the remote, Lem. On the air in five; got about three, maybe four minutes."

Lem Perrish took the count to steady his breathing, then spoke into the microphone held in his good hand. "This is Lem Perrish reporting for Radio Free Metro. I'd give you our location, but why make it easier for the PSF? They'll have a triangulation on our position soon enough. PSF tanks are moving into the downtown area along all major arteries now. The is the first time tanks have actually entered the city since, on the orders of Presidential Security

Advisor Hobart Townes, the blockade that now totally encircles Metro began, some six days ago. The resistance to the tanks is at once overwhelming in its spirit and pitiful in its effectiveness."

Men and women were pouring into the streets now, as they had been for the last several minutes, most of them bare handed.

"In a country where citizens were once guaranteed the legal right to be armed for defense of life and liberty, those citizens of Metro who haven't joined the ranks of the collaborators are reduced to fighting back with bricks and chunks of paving materials and baseball bats, against machine-gun-equipped tanks and assault-rifle-armed soldiers. So far, no shots have been fired."

Perrish raised his binoculars. "Yes. The soldiers of the Presidential Strike Force are donning gas masks now and the hatches atop the tanks are being sealed shut. One can only assume this is in preparation for firing—yes! Clouds of gray-white smoke—it must be a type of tear gas—are billowing from flame-thrower–like spray units carried on the backs of some of the PSF personnel.

"I see a human chain forming, at least a hundred men and women linking arms to block the street as the tanks advance toward them. Will they stop? Will the men and women forming that human chain be able to withstand the tear gas?"

Perrish was getting the signal that their time was running out.

And he heard a burst of automatic-weapons fire.

"My God. . . . That—wait—Someone—it had to have been one of the PSF personnel, because none of the Metro citizens appears to be armed and it was full-automatic assualt-rifle fire. Yes. Two men"—Perrish raised the binoculars — "make that one man and a woman, down in the street.

The chain is breaking, but not retreating. I'm seeing courage and rage, ladies and gentlemen, driving the citizens of Metro to attack armed men and tanks with nothing but bricks and rocks and clubs. This is like Hungary in—"

More gunfire, louder this time because there was so much of it, machine guns from several of the tanks. They seemed to be firing over the heads of the demonstrators.

Bricks were being thrown at the PSF personnel. Some of the PSF personnel in the leading ranks carried transparent riot shields, but many of those carrying them threw them down, bringing their rifles up into firing positions.

Someone attacked three armed PSF men; his only apparent weapon, as Perrish watched through the binoculars, was a baseball bat. He was shot down.

Now the gunfire was general, the demonstrators falling into the street, others running for their lives, some stopping to hurtle their bricks or brandish their baseball bats. More gunfire.

"The PSF have opened fire. I can see at least a dozen people down in the streets. Gunfire rocks the air around me, echoes and reechoes along the canyons of the downtown area. The tanks are speeding up. My God—a tank has just run over the bodies of three Metro citizens from among the demonstrators. One of the tanks—its turret is twisting. No!" There was an explosion, earsplittingly loud, the microphone whistling with it as Perrish tried to come back. "I —the gun mounted atop the tank has fired, the cannon round impacting the first floor of Mercer Brothers department store, flames rising within the building now where only seconds before some of the demonstrators fled for shelter."

"We gotta get outa here, Lem. Now. They got us!"

Perrish nodded. "Fighting is everywhere. More machine guns are opening up. I'm seeing dozens killed or wounded.

My engineer tells me they have a triangulation on us now and we have to withdraw. But we'll be back, broadcasting the truth until they catch us and someone replaces us. The truth will make us free. This is Radio Free Metro, Lem Perrish signing off."

"Outa here!"

Perrish dropped to his knees beside his friend, helping him fold up shop. He could hear the droning of helicopters in the distance.

Maybe they'd waited too long.

Chapter Seven

AFTER LETTING HER take the mandatory look at his arm, Matthew Smith had insisted on her rubbing down Araby before doing anything further for him. She'd obeyed him, then found him on the floor of the cabin, passed out.

Matthew Smith was about six feet tall and well built. He looked to be about 175 pounds, but was a little over 200 and getting him off the floor and onto the couch was all but impossible for her. But Lilly Twobears did it anyway. Once he was on the couch, she unbuckled his gun belt, rolled him over slightly, and pulled it free of him.

She got off his coat without cutting it—it would be hard enough to repair the tear in the left sleeve from the bullet—and felt the odd heaviness in his pocket. She looked. It was his little automatic that he carried as a hideout gun, the hammer fully cocked and the safety applied. Carefully, she removed the gun and set it on the coffee table. Then she set to removing his sweater. For that she simply used his big black pocket knife—she'd found it where he'd flipped it into the snow—and severed the seam running up the left rib cage and along the underside of the left sleeve, and then, with the garment free of his injured left arm, pulled the rest of it over his head and off his right arm and put it on the floor. The shirt took a little doing, cutting the sleeve off at the seam so she could repair it later. He never wore undershirts.

The gunshot wound in his left upper arm was a deep graze over the tricep and must have hurt him terribly; but, as far as she could tell, had bled itself clean. He'd had a tetanus shot three months ago after cutting himself on a nail while fixing one of the stalls at their old place; and he was generally healthy. There was little fear of infection. She got clean bandages, hot water, and antiseptic and attended the wound, uncertain whether he slept from exhaustion or had passed out with the pain.

She draped the afghan over him, then knelt by his feet and began pulling off his boots so she could make him more comfortable.

Matthew opened his eyes. "I take it that I'm alive."

"You take it correctly."

He started to sit up before she could tell him not to and then said, "Why did you let me do that?" as he leaned back, his right hand closing over his eyes.

"Before you ask, I took care of Araby. Walked her for a few minutes, rubbed her down, fed and watered her. You got blood on your saddle, but I'll clean it off."

"I can—"

"No, you can't. By the time you could get to it, it'll be set."

She went back to removing his boots.

"I can—"

"No, you can't. Exert yourself too much and you'll start bleeding again."

"You saved my life."

"Hardly. I just saved you from getting into contact with that dog."

"I disagree."

"Don't worry about the dogs. I'll take care of the bodies."

"You can leave them—"

"No, I can't. They'll just attract other animals. I'll drag them together and burn them."

"Then take my pistol; you really are terrible with that shotgun."

"All right. Are you in any pain?"

"I could use something to eat."

"I'll feed you in a little while. Do you think you lost so much blood that a drink would hurt?" She looked up at him from where she knelt and he smiled. "I'll get you a glass of wine. Better for you than whiskey." His feet were like ice, even though his socks were dry.

She stood up and moved quickly toward the kitchen. Taking down a glass from the inverted rack over the counter that he'd built for her, she poured a healthy draft of port for him, closed the bottle, and brought the glass back to him. He took it, downed a full quarter of the glass, and leaned his head back.

She sat down at the foot of the couch, drew his feet up onto her lap, and started removing his socks.

"What are you—"

"Your feet feel like ice. How's your right knee?"

"Stiff."

"You need a good soak in the tub."

"Later."

"Agreed," she told him, both of his socks off now. She pulled up her sweater and tugged the front of the blouse beneath it from the waistband of her skirt and brought his feet up under her clothes, the soles against her bare abdomen. She winced with the sudden touch of cold flesh, but not so loudly that she thought he would have heard. "That feel warmer?"

"Yes. You're a fine woman."

"You've told me that before."

"That train Wisdom saw. There were men and women

aboard it. From the clothes, military. I saw one of them get shot to death. It's a camp of some sort. There's a lot of heavy equipment going up there. Tanks. It's a fortress, impenetrable for all intents and purposes."

"How did you get shot, Smith?" Lilly asked him.

"Tactical error. Not much of a gunshot wound, is it?" He craned his neck and looked at his upper arm.

"Not much of a gunshot wound. You should feel a lot stronger in a day or so." His feet were finally starting to warm, which was doubly good because her teeth were close to chattering. "I'll make us a good hot dinner in a little while." Matthew downed more of the port. "Go easy on the wine. I'm looking forward to stimulating dinner conversation."

"You may be disappointed." He laughed, his whole face, seams and wrinkles and day-old stubble, lighting with it.

"I'll risk it. Sleep while I take care of things."

"I can—"

"No." She stood up, wrapped his feet in the afghan, and set about doing what she had to do.

Matthew Smith was asleep before she left the cabin.

Chapter Eight

HE RECOGNIZED THE face. Ricardo Montenegro had the kind of a face that wasn't easily forgotten. In his youth, it was conjectured in the dossier Kearney'd seen once in London, Montenegro must have contracted smallpox. The marks of it were all over his face, but despite his pitted forehead, cheeks, and chin, Montenegro was so undeniably handsome that Kearney gave equal weight to Montenegro's looks and Montenegro's money and power for the half-dozen women who encircled him, giggling, smiling, preening, fawning over him.

"Ricardo. I want you to meet somebody." Montenegro turned around immediately when Borsoi spoke, a fact Geoffrey Kearney filed away for later analysis. "This is Thad Borden."

"Good to meet you, amigo." Montenegro smiled, extending his right hand.

Kearney took it, the handclasp firm and warm and dry, everything that a handshake could convey—strength, assuredness, the offer of friendship—compressed within it. "Pleasure to meet ya," Kearney said.

Their eyes held one another's for what had to be seconds only but seemed longer to Kearney, the genteel noise of the party drowned out in the look.

"I think Thad's the man I've been looking for," Borsoi told Montenegro.

"Good. I know how long you've been looking."

"A little rough around the edges." Borsoi grinned, clapping Kearney on the shoulder good-naturedly. "Sort of diamond in the rough, but worth it."

The handshake broke.

Montenegro, with a glance at the women, dismissed them into the party, Montenegro, Borsoi, and Kearney standing almost shoulder to shoulder in a triangle.

The party was as unlike the party almost a week before at the other beach house as an orgy was from a royal ball. Aside from himself and Reefer, who was almost always in attendance, none of the others in what Kearney loosely catalogued as Borsoi's immediate "gang" were present, except enough of the women to keep things lively, Linda among them.

Rather than half-stoned young hoodlums, this smaller, more sedate gathering included a number of foreigners, almost as sharply dressed in expensive casual clothes as was Montenegro, and a number of locals: the county sheriff, his chief deputy, a judge, several businessmen, and even one face recognizable from the Metro news media. A tape of some of Chopin's preludes played softly as a background to the conversation and most of the alcohol being consumed was champagne.

"You're staring at my face," Montenegro said, the smile flickering out of his eyes for a moment, then returning. "When I was a boy, I was very ill and nearly died. This is what the illness left me." He waved his right hand across his face, then picked up a fresh glass of champagne from one of the girls circulating about the room. All of the girls, except for Linda and Borsoi's own women, were dressed in skimpy little lingerie-shop French-maid outfits, some of them actually serving drinks and hors d'oeuvres. Kearney had seen one of the girls with a silver tray, on it neatly razor-bladed lines of cocaine and piles of color-coordinated pills, Quaaludes and the like.

"What is so very special about Thad here, Dimitri?"

Borsoi laughed softly. "I don't want him to get a swelled head, but I've never seen a man handle himself so well. And he thinks before he opens his mouth; always something going on behind his eyes. And, he's got the look as well. Charisma is important. We'll get professionals in, of course, to coach his diction, find the right style of clothes for him, all of that. But, he's perfect."

Kearney looked at Borsoi. This was all new to him. So he said, "I don't follow you, Mr. Johnson."

"Call me Dimitri, Thad."

"Yeah. What, ahh—"

Montenegro sipped at his champagne. "You see, Thad, for some time—well, Dimitri, you could explain it better, I'm sure."

Borsoi chuckled a little, his eyes following one of the girls in the French-maid outfits, then said, "It's very simple. The Front for the Liberation of North America needs a front man, someone with whom the people here can identify, a leader who looks like a typical American, who has charisma, can win the hearts and minds of the populace. Now, with Roman Makowski's policies so seriously dividing the country, the FLNA can become a symbol of unity.

"But," Borsoi continued, "to effect this unification, we need a special man, someone the people here will come to love and respect and trust—trust is most important. We'll fabricate a background out of a real man's past, then with a new name and the right appearance and the right words, that man will be followed, respected, admired.

"Congratulations, Thad," Borsoi told Geoffrey Kearney.

"We have chosen you as the new leader of the Front for the Liberation of North America."

Borsoi extended his hand.

Kearney took it, not knowing at all what else to do.

Chapter Nine

DAVID HOLDEN SNAPPED back the PSF guard's head and raked the Defender knife across the man's exposed throat, averting his eyes from the blood spray.

All of them were playing a dangerous game now, and one thing Holden insisted upon for the Patriots to minimize at least part of the risk was that they wear durable gloves and protect their skin from unnecessary exposure when involved in any sort of mission during that might involve spilling blood at close range. And no knife that was used in combat was ever to be clenched in the teeth. The people who wanted to look like some macho image out of a pirate movie could ship out and fight the FLNA and the PSF on their own.

The risk of infection from human blood was not great, but when punching someone in the mouth there was always a danger of skinning one's own knuckles while at the same time drawing the adversary's blood, and there was no sense in taking even a small chance on slow and torturous death. From what little he knew beyond the ordinary precautions, much of the medical research that had been under way to stem the tide of Acquired Immune Deficiency Syndrome had all but ground to a halt.

As with any war the noncombatants suffered the most.

As Holden drew the body back into the gap between the two parked cars, he tapped on the push-to-talk button of his radio, giving the brief Morse signal—two dashes, a dot followed by three dashes—for "Go."

Holden wiped the excess blood from his knife against the dead man's trouser leg.

Rapidly but carefully, Holden searched the PSF man's body for papers, finding none, then relieved the body of useful items like the Beretta M9 pistol, the spare magazines for it, the first-aid kit, et cetera. With the exception of the pistol which he shoved in his belt, he placed all the other items into the black rucksack he took from his back.

Reshouldering the rucksack, Holden picked up the dead man's rifle and slung it across his own back beside the rucksack. Rosie and the others hadn't reached him yet, so Holden took the time to remove the dead man's boots. There were Patriots going into combat in track shoes and cowboy boots, and genuine military-issue boots were at a premium. Laces, however, were not a problem yet. With the Defender knife Holden cut the laces away and tugged off the boots.

His nostrils were assailed immediately by strong foot odor, but the boots could be sanitized.

As Rosie and the others joined him, Holden handed her the boots. He could see her bandana creasing where she wrinkled up her nose. She took the boots and placed them in the rucksack on Holden's back.

Holden, with hand signals, pointed out the positions of the other two PSF guards on this side of the parking lot's perimeter. The PSF had moved in only hours ago and was relying on human security and conventional trip wires, easy enough to get around.

Unsheathing the Defender knife, Holden scribed into the dirt the layout of the trip-wire system.

Rosie drew the knife she'd adopted. It was a curious-looking instrument, the blade's leading edge like that of a tanto, a Bowie-like recurve behind the leading edge and the blade thickness more like that of a crowbar.

Holden indicated, with hand signals again, that he would take the man on the right.

Rosie had the one in the middle and Patsy Alfredi the one on the far left.

Holden looked at his watch.

As the Rolex's sweep second hand crossed over the inverted triangle that was the symbol for twelve, Holden signaled they move out. Unless something had gone wrong, Steel, LeFleur, Runningdeer, and Blumenthal would be in position, ready to hit the perimeter on the far side of the lot.

Holden gave Rosie a wink and started forward in a low crouch. . . .

Rose Shepherd crept forward on hands and knees, the only way, given the limited cover, to get close enough to do the job. The knife in her hand was an option only, if for some reason the man she was stalking should turn around unexpectedly. And, she promised herself, when this was all over, if ever it was and she lived to see freedom in the United States again, she'd never kill with a knife again. Hands, feet, gun, club, no problem if the situation called for it. And she liked knives, especially this Big Ugly One she'd come by from the Miami Metro/Dade Patriot leader's daughter. But killing with a knife was something that chilled her just thinking about it.

Behind a Volkswagen Fox, dropping almost flat, she unlimbered the Barnett Commando crossbow with which she'd been practicing for the past several weeks. She'd oiled the hinges of the cocking mechanism so they wouldn't squeak. Now she drew up into a crouch and butted the

Commando into the ground at the edge of the macadam blacktop of the parking lot.

She cocked the crossbow, closed it, then reached into the quiver at her belt, nocking a broadhead hunting bolt.

The only way to reliably take out someone in silence with the Commando, as she understood it, was to sever the spinal column. And the best place for that was the neck, because, aside from the spine being most exposed there, there was added insurance in that the bolt would at the same time sever the spine and penetrate the windpipe, thus doubly obviating the chance for a cry.

She would have used the knife, but she couldn't get close enough. And she was glad.

She rose to a kneeling position overlooking the VW's rear bumper, the sentry with his back to her.

She brought the Commando to her shoulder, settling the open sights. At the distance, a scope was unnecessary.

She thumbed off the safety.

She inhaled, let a portion of her breath out, locked the rest in her throat, and touched the trigger.

There was a soft thrumming sound and the PSF sentry's arms began to move toward his neck and he fell flat on his face with the bolt polking out of the rear of his neck, the only sound other than that of his body hitting the tarmac the sound of his rifle clanging softly against the hard surface.

She reslung the crossbow, caught up her M-16, and moved out. . . .

From his position beneath the trailer of an eighteen-wheeler at the edge of the parking lot, David Holden could see the sentry as he fell to Rosie's crossbow.

Holden wriggled around, peered round the tires on his immediate right, and watched as Patsy Alfredi put down the third sentry with a Chinese cleaver. Holden glanced left. The dead man whose weapons and boots he'd taken an instant before lay beside him.

Two men in less than ten minutes, up close with a knife. Holden wondered if he were losing it, because it didn't disgust him quite enough to make him want to throw up.

There was no time to worry about it.

He checked his watch.

Steel and his men should be through with the sentry removal on the far perimeter. He waited for the Morse signal to be made by opening and closing the frequency on his belt radio.

And, in the next instant, it came.

Holden spoke this time into the radio. "Hit. I say again, hit!"

David Holden heard the sound of Blumenthal's grenade launcher, rolled from beneath the eighteen-wheeler, and tore a grenade from his web gear, lobbing it, as he stood, toward the concentration of PSF personnel nearest him.

As the grenade went airborne, Holden swung his M-16 forward, gunfire already rattling from across the parking lot. . . .

Rose Shepherd's M-16 bucked in her hands as she sprayed out a half-magazineful of 5.56mm ball into three men standing beside the nearest of the PSF armor, an APC. All three men went down, only one feebly returning fire as he fell.

She ran toward the APC, taking cover beside it as the level of gunfire swelled on all sides of her. A half dozen more of the Patriot cells members were onto the field, moving in a wedge to close with her, their M-16's firing.

The Metro Patriot Cell's solitary mortar began firing now, the scream of the mortar round over her head. She tucked down, the impact coming. As she looked beyond the APC, one of the enemy tanks was missing part of a tread and a staff car was overturned and on fire, half into a smallish crater near the center of the parking lot.

From the east end of the field she could see the truck, one of Mitch Diamond's eighteen-wheelers, bouncing off the road and onto the tarmac, doing sixty at least. . . .

David Holden was up, running, shouting into his radio, "Phase Two! I say again, Phase Two!" Another mortar round came and Holden involuntarily ducked. The Patriots needed rockets, more mortars, more of everything. He kept running, the mortar round exploding as he neared the closest of the tanks. A man was in cover near the turret, trying to move through the tank's open hatchway. Holden stabbed the M-16 toward him and fired a long burst, then another, the man's body rocking back, his pistol discharging twice into the air as he fell.

Holden let the M-16 drop to his side and vaulted onto the tread; clambering over onto the body of the tank and toward the hatchway.

The tank started to move and the hatchway to close, as the turret began turning.

David Holden reached to his web gear with both hands, snatching a gas grenade and a high explosive, letting the spoons snap away, counting seconds on the one with the lesser delay. He lobbed both grenades through the hatchway just as it was nearly closed.

He was up, moving, a rumbling in the tank beneath him as he jumped clear, then a second rumbling, louder than the first. As Holden hit the tarmac in a flex, rolled, and looked back, the tank seemed to jump slightly and then came to a dead stop.

The eighteen-wheeler was nearly to the midway point of

the parking lot, where the greatest concentration of tanks, trucks, and support vehicles was assembled, and the greatest number of PSF personnel. Bullets ricocheted off the eighteen-wheeler's cab, the windshield spiderwebbing, the entire driver's-side West Coast mirror shot away.

"Fire support for the truck. I repeat. Fire support for the truck!"

Holden took up cover beside the stalled tank, firing his M-16 from the shoulder. He could see the results of Blumenthal's Hawk MM-1 grenade launcher, portions of vehicles going airborne, portions of bodies too.

The eighteen-wheeler's air brakes screeched wildly, the cab skidding slightly, the trailer starting to jacknife. Before the vehicle was completely stopped, the driver's-side door swung open and Mitch Diamond, the left sleeve of his gray jacket soaked with blood and some sort of a head wound evident near his left temple, jumped clear, running, stumbling in a fusilade of automatic-weapons fire, then running on.

Holden had a fresh stick up the M-16's magazine well, spraying it into largest concentration of PSF personnel.

He was counting off the seconds until the explosives secreted inside the truck's trailer detonated. He gave it eighty-three seconds more.

Mitch Diamond fell.

Holden started to bolt from cover to get him, but he saw Rosie beating him to it, her M-16's muzzle making a continuous tongue of muzzle flash as she ran. A grenade was thrown. Holden brought the M-16 to his shoulder and fired it out, trying—uselessly, he realized—to hit it.

The grenade fell to the tarmac, rolled, Rosie throwing herself left and away as the grenade detonated. "Cover me for no more than thirty seconds, then evacuate," Holden said into his handset. When the explosives in the truck went—a shower of debris rained down over Rosie and Mitch. Holden ran, toward Rosie, Rosie already stumbling to her feet, lurching toward Mitch Diamond, her M-16 firing again.

Holden dumped the magazine in his assault rifle, replaced it with a fresh one, dropped half into a crouch, and fired toward three PSF troopers charging toward Rosie and Mitch Diamond. Holden killed one and put a second one down, uncertain of whether the man was dead or merely wounded. Gunfire plowed into the tarmac near Holden's feet.

Holden fired again, the last remaining man of the three firing at him.

Holden emptied the M-16.

The PSF trooper fell.

As Holden went to change magazines, he could see Rosie, Mitch Diamond's right arm across her shoulders, half dragging him to his feet.

Holden completed the magazine change as he ran, intercepting Rosie and Mitch. "You all right?"

"Ears ring and I'm dirty as hell," Rosie Shepherd shouted back.

"We've got maybe fifty seconds. Five-oh seconds." Holden took Mitch Diamond up over his shoulder, into a fireman's carry, handing over the M-16 from his right hand to Rosie. Holden drew the larger Beretta from the crossdraw holster at his waist, triggering two shots from his left hand into a group of four PSF men coming at them from behind the nearest APC.

Rosie, an M-16 in each hand, fired, mowing down two of the men, the other two retreating to cover.

As best he could, David Holden ran. Mitch Diamond, a big man, hung over his shoulders like a sack of wet cement.

Forty seconds, maybe less, until detonation.

Holden could hear grenades exploding from behind him and realized it had to be Blumenthal disobeying orders and covering their withdrawal.

Thirty seconds.

Gunfire from behind them, very heavy.

Rosie broke off, Holden glancing back once as she fired out both M-16's, taking down another two men, possibly three.

Holden's lungs ached, the exertion of carrying Mitch Diamond beating him down. He kept running.

Twenty seconds, maybe less.

The pickups and vans the Metro Patriots had driven to the target area in were pulling out along the road beyond the parking lot, gunfire coming from the truck beds and through the open side doors. One of the vans slowed, two others veering off. Steel and LeFleur were jumping out of the nearest of the vans, LeFleur with an Uzi in both hands, firing to cover their escape, Steel running toward Holden.

"Give me Diamond!"

Holden ran, meeting Steel a hundred yards from the van. "No time. Cover us!" Steel swung his M-16 up. As Holden glanced back, Steel and LeFleur, with Rosie between them, were laying down fire toward a group of five vehicles speeding across the parking lot, two of the vehicles APCS, one a tank, the other two small trucks.

Holden reached the van, Runningdeer putting down an M-16 and helping to haul Diamond's semiconscious form inside.

Ten seconds.

Rosie, Steel, and LeFleur were running for the van, which Patsy Alfredi was already getting into motion.

"Where the hell's Blumenthal?"

"He's on another truck. I just got word," she shouted back.

The van was moving steadily now, LeFleur throwing himself aboard, Runningdeer grabbing for him.

Steel and Rosie were running alongside, Steel suddenly grabbing Rosie up by the waist and shouting, "David! Catch!" Steel launched her forward and Holden reached for her, catching her by the pistol belt and the front of her field jacket, Rosie's left hand on the grab handle.

Holden rolled back with her, dragging her inside.

Steel jumped, hit the floor of the van, and rolled.

No seconds left.

There was a brilliant flash of yellow light, and the eighteen-wheeler wasn't there anymore, a black-and-orange fireball belching rapidly skyward.

Holden let go of Rosie and dived for the sliding door, slamming it shut as the rain of shrapnel started, a pinging on all sides of the van as though suddenly they were in a hailstorm. The windshield shattered. Before Holden could check, Patsy Alfredi shouted, "I'm all right!"

Inside the eighteen-wheeler's trailer they had loaded more than a ton of scrap metal.

The truck, with the modest amount of explosives, but with the extra five hundred gallons of gasoline and the junkyard shrapnel, was a giant grenade.

Bill Runningdeer said it. "Scratch one new PSF base."

Chapter Ten

HE'D NEVER GOTTEN the bath the night before, nor awakened for much more dinner than some soup that Lilly had
fed him. Wrapping a plastic bag over the bandage on his
upper arm, he'd showered, after sleeping for better than
sixteen hours straight, his knee stiff and his arm stiff.

But, as always, the knee had worked itself out by the
time he was out of the shower. The plastic bag had done
little to protect the bandage, but Lilly changed the bandage
for him, as she'd said she would have anyway. As he sat
down—he was weak still—and picked up his coffee, he
watched Lilly moving about the kitchen.

Her hair, the color of a raven's wings, as poets sometimes put it, hung in one very thick, very long braid down
her back, reaching almost to the bow that tied her apron
about her waist.

He could smell the steak and potatoes cooking as he
raised the cup to his lips, the strong black coffee overpow-
ering the other, equally pleasant kitchen smells.

"Thank you," Smith said to Lilly Twobears as she set a
plate down before him, the steak, the eggs—sunny-side up
just the way he liked them—and a neat mound of cottage-
fried potatoes the most appetizing meal he'd ever seen. Re-
alistically, part of the basis for that feeling was the fact that
he had not eaten in something like thirty hours and had

pushed himself beyond what he'd thought were his current limits.

"How are you feeling?" Lilly smiled.

"Well enough."

"For what?"

Matthew Smith looked at her as he sampled the eggs, put down his fork, sipped at his coffee, then took up fork and knife to attack the small steak. "I'll have to drive down the mountain and see Bob today. Bob needs to be told about what's going on at Widow's Table, so he can get his Patriots up there and they can all die uselessly."

"That's a terrible thing to say! And anyway, Bob called on the radio. He's coming here. 'Die uselessly.' "

"When I was in law enforcement, I went through SWAT training, Lilly. And, before that, I was in the Marine Corps, as you well know. In the Marine Corps they were still teaching the frontal assault and good men were dying using it in Vietnam. The Marshals Service SWAT instructors taught that you approached stealthily and got into the perfect position, or as close to it as you could. Two extremes of tactical philosophy. Basically, neither system will work against the objective in question, and certainly not the frontal assault, the only tactic Bob seems to know how to order. Widow's Table is all but impenetrable."

Smith tasted his steak. It was excellent, as Lilly's cooking invariably was.

" 'All but impenetrable'?"

"Yes. With the right personnel some stealthy means could be exploited, I suppose, but such a plan would require vastly more sophisticated personnel than Bob's ten little Indian boys." He cut more of the steak, speared a slice of potato onto the fork with the steak, and marinated both for an instant in the runny yellow of his eggs.

"I hate it when you talk like that!" Lilly looked down at her coffee, not drinking it. "It makes you sound as if—"

"I am prejudiced against Indians?" He ate the steak, potato, and egg mixture, then set down his fork. "Hardly. What I'm prejudiced against, as you very well know, is incompetence. That is why when I wanted to become involved with military service, I chose the Marines, and when I wanted to become involved in law enforcement I chose the Marshals Service. Both are the best at what they do. Bob and his Patriots are quite sincere; if sincerity were the measure of potential for success, Bob and his men would indeed be the best. But sincerity doesn't cut it. That they would make a valiant, even noble effort, is as undeniable as it is obvious. That they would fail in such an effort is equally undeniable and, unfortunately, equally obvious. No. They would go to Widow's Table and they would surely die, accomplishing nothing."

Lilly held the mug of coffee in both hands. She was very beautiful, and he was sorry that he was so upsetting her. But the truth was the truth and no amount of dancing around the truth would make it any less true. "What exactly is up there?" she asked.

Smith continued eating for a moment, taking a bite of his toast. Lilly grabbed it from his hand, took a bite, passed it back to him. "Do you want some toast?"

"No, I'm not hungry," she said.

"Oh." Smith nodded. He took a swallow of his coffee, then set the cup down. "You wanted to know what I saw yesterday at Widow's Table," Smith began. . . .

Bob was a slightly built man whom some would call wiry. He reminded her always of Alan Ladd, which was silly because he was more "Indian" looking than she was and Alan Ladd had been blond and fair complexioned.

But Bob still reminded her of him.

Although Matthew looked a little weak, still, he seemed to exude a restless vigor few other men—Bob and the three Patriots who'd accompanied him included—possessed at full strength.

Matthew Smith leaned a little too heavily against the mantle, a cigar clamped in his teeth, listening while Bob spoke. "So, they just shot this man? An Army officer?"

"I believe he was Army, yes."

"In cold blood."

"Dead is the operative term."

"And you're saying we can't get up there without getting killed."

"No, Bob, what I am saying is that you cannot get up there at all. You'll get yourselves killed long before you ever near the facility."

"Fuck that shit," Ed Greyeagle snapped.

Lilly looked at Matthew. Matthew, holding his cigar in his right hand now, looked almost pityingly at Ed. "In this house which Lilly and I share, language such as that is not tolerated, Greyeagle. Again and you wait in the car."

Ed Greyeagle—she'd gone to reservation school with him—looked away and lit a cigarette.

Bob asked, "Then what would you recommend that we do?"

Matthew waited for a moment to answer—seemed to be studying the glowing tip of his cigar as if it would provide him with inspiration. He looked up from the cigar, directly at Bob, and said, "A commando unit, if it were comprised of the right people with the right equipment and could avail itself of battle dress utilities similar to those worn by the Presidential Strike Force and appropriate unit insignia, could, under the right carefully constructed circumstances, hijack the train somewhere between Fort Devon and Widow's Table. That is assuming, of course, a suitable engineer can be found to operate the train. That way, at least, it would be possible to get inside."

Henry Blackdog, who still looked a great deal more like a certified public accountant than a freedom fighter, looked up from his pipe, asking, "And just where do you suppose we find such a commando unit, Smith?"

Matthew smiled at Blackdog, nodding his head as he said, "Indeed, Henry, that does represent a bit of a challenge. However, such a force does seem to exist. Like anyone, I've been hearing a great deal about the Patriot cell in operation around Metro."

"That's a coupla thousand—"

"Two thousand, one hundred seventy-eight miles, to be exact, calculated from the center of Metro to Fort Devon, Greyeagle. This Professor Holden and his people would seem to be the best of the Patriots."

Bob said it and Lilly shivered. "Would you accompany them, assuming we could get them, Smith?"

Matthew looked at her. She nodded, knowing he would do what he wanted anyway.

"Yes."

Chapter Eleven

THERE WAS A swirl of snow all around the honor guard as they waited at ease; the wind always seemed to howl cyclonically here atop Widow's Table—and very cold. One of the locals who was cooperating with the small garrison stationed outside the town of Fort Devon had explained that the mesa on which their Fort Makowski was set was called Widow's Table because the early explorers, mountain men, had been struck by the mesa's desolation, like something abandoned in death.

Local color was interesting enough, Hackler supposed, but all it was was an excuse to sell souvenir maps and fake Indian moccasins and cowboy lariats.

Hackler watched the sky, waiting for the helicopter.

There was no sign of it yet, so he returned to his musings.

The whole place—the boring little town of Fort Devon, the surrounding countryside—was like something out of a low-budget western, lots of cowboys and lots of Indians and lots of open spaces and nothing of interest.

"Lieutenant Colonel Eugene Lewis Hackler," he barely whispered under his breath. It had a nice ring to it, much better than Federal Prisoner Hackler, E.L., No. 104 32 9879. Perhaps that was why this place, Fort Makowski, was still so uncomfortable for him.

There was so much openness surrounding him that

sometimes, when he considered it, he would experience a mild wave of dizziness, an unease in his stomach, a gasping for breath as cold gripped him. It was something like the descriptions of vertigo he had read about in books.

Hackler told himself this would pass.

With time almost everything did.

He could see the helicopter, felt a smile cross his lips. He should have been wearing a white suit rather than his PSF battle dress utilities. And there should have been a little person with a French accent, running up to him, shouting, "The plane! The plane!"

Hackler was a master of television reruns, everything from Lucy's various incarnations to animated automobiles that turned into robot avengers.

He'd read a lot of books.

He'd watched a great deal of TV.

"Major. Call the honor guard to attention and give them parade rest until Director Townes steps off the chopper."

"Yes, sir!"

The major reissued the orders to the captain and the captain in turn . . . It seemed to go on ad infinitum.

With no family to whom he could write letters, or friends who came to visit on those rare days when such was allowed, the television in the day room had been his best companion. And the majority of the men there had imbecilic tastes, so often his viewing fare was less to his liking than to that of some of his fellows. At least in the early days, until he had realized that prison was the most basic sort of governmental system: rule of the strong.

He'd become one of the strong, so strong that if he wanted to watch a sitcom while someone was watching a soap he just turned to it and no one said a word, so strong that if he wanted to shut the television off so he could read or think or just to demonstrate that he could, he did it.

Life imprisonment. He'd served five years and might have been out on parole in another two; but then the representative of Hobart Townes had sent for him, and in the middle of the night he'd been driven to a crossroads, changed cars, and been offered a drink and a cigar and a new chance. "You killed a man during an armory robbery. Did you do it intentionally?"

"No."

"Why did you do it, then?"

"It needed doing. He had a gun pointed at me."

"Couldn't you have dropped your weapon?"

"No. I didn't want to get caught."

"You did very well in the military. Eight years. Why did you leave? You were an officer."

"Dead-end job. Not enough money."

"Would you kill again?"

"Is that an offer?"

The man had only smiled.

Hackler, once a captain, was given credit for his time since separation and promoted to lieutenant colonel with a regular Army commission to the Presidential Strike Force.

Life was perverse.

The helicopter was landing.

The snow swirled more violently.

"Company!"

"Platoon!"

"Ten-hut!"

Hackler drew himself to something like attention, tugged at his pistol belt—he carried one of the new Beretta M-9's on each hip, something quite the fashion among ranking officers in the PSF—and started toward the aircraft.

He smiled, still wishing some little man would call out, "The plane!"

Chapter Twelve

SMITH'S LEFT ARM was stiff at his side, but it felt worse when he left it in the sling Lilly had improvised. His Stetson low over his eyes and screwed down tight against the wind-driven snow, he crossed the yard toward the stable. Where Lilly had buried the feral dogs that had attacked Araby, he could not say, because there had been several inches of fresh snowfall overnight and all signs of what had transpired were obscured.

He flexed his fingers inside his glove, his left arm paining him a little as he did, but he reasoned that the more he worked it, the sooner it would be back to normal. And he noticed the sleeve of his jacket. Except for three lines barely thicker than the width of a human hair, there was no sign the sheepskin-lined leather jacket had ever been damaged.

"Remarkable," he said under his breath as he approached the stable door.

He entered, passing the other horses and immediately going to Araby's stall. She came forward, nuzzling her head against his right hand. As he opened his hand, she snatched the two lumps of sugar he'd brought for her. "If I thought you were only interested in me for my sugar, well —but of course, you love me for myself, don't you, Araby?" And he grabbed roughly at her mane, shook her a little, then clapped her on the side of the neck. She ducked her head for him to stroke along her forehead between her eyes, something she'd always liked.

All creatures were creatures of habit.

He did what she wanted, his mind elsewhere. Being with Araby—she was so basic—often cleared his mind when it was more important than usual to think something through carefully.

Smith had committed himself.

If—

And, the "if" was a very big one: getting a substantial number of the Metro Patriot Cell members to embark on the comparatively dangerous trip cross country to carry out the commando mission that Bob and his Patriot cell were incapable of carrying out successfully on their own.

And, of course, there was the other side of the coin.

Smith rubbed his hand back on his head. "You want more sugar, huh?" He found more, gave the last two lumps to Araby, and stroked her between the eyes some more.

If the Metro Patriot Cell personnel were unwilling or unable to come, of course something still had to be done about the men and women being held atop Widow's Table.

Which meant, in the final analysis, he would get together with Bob and his men and they would try a simplified plan so there would be at least some chance, however modest or improbable, of success. And, in the end, they would die or be captured.

All his life he had attempted to escape the inevitable, and with good success.

This time he might not be able to accomplish that.

"I envy you, in a way," Smith told Araby. "But, of course, an abdication of responsibility brings along with it an abdication of thought. So, it's best that you are a horse and I am a man.

"At least for you," Smith told her, stroking her forehead.

Chapter Thirteen

THE EFFECT WAS like staring down into two unyielding and massive breasts, seen from the inside out. Amusement with such images allayed Hackler's agitation, but only for the briefest instant. He was, after all, the jailer, yet the very thought of that depressed him, unnerved him. To kill men, however it was done, did not disturb him. But to confine men as he had once been confined offended his soul.

The smooth gray concrete pits were hemispherical. Their sides were so steeply dished from their center bases some thirty feet below the metal grilled catwalk that nearly all of the prisoners were crowded into the centers in one manner or another. The drain holes at the centers approximated the nipples to match his earlier fleeting impression.

There were vastly more bodies within the pit to their left, where the male prisoners—substantially outnumbering captured female officers—were interned. The men, in their pit, were forced to rest against those closer to the center in order to maintain their balance, because standing on such radically sloping sides was physically impossible.

To the right side of the catwalk, at the approximate center of which Hackler and his VIP tourist, Hobart Townes, had stopped in the inspection tour, were the women in their identical hemispherical prison. The women, because of their drastically smaller numbers, were better able to position themselves with some degree of comfort. Nor, Hackler realized, did pride keep them from huddling close to one another for warmth.

Townes's eyes had a peculiar light in them as his gaze passed over the women, a smile curling the corners of his mouth slightly. Then Townes's eyes shifted toward the men again, and Hackler's eyes followed.

The cots were all at the center, and several men sat stiffly on each cot, while the rest stood around awkwardly or tried moving to heat up body circulation. Very few—the ones who looked in the generally poorest health—sat on the concrete. It seemed to radiate cold upward, and Hackler shivered involuntarily.

He gestured down into the pit. "The cream of the crap, Mr. Townes," Eugene Hackler said after a moment, trying to brighten his mood, his breath steaming as he spoke. "From among all those arrested who were not executed for one reason or another, these are the ones most dangerous because they were most loyal to the old regime. And they're powerless to do anything but wait for whatever we have in store for them. We keep the temperatures just low enough that they are never exactly comfortable. The lower temperatures help to demoralize them, as was suggested in your guidelines, Mr. Townes; and, we've also found that the prisoners are overall less physically resistant. Blankets are given to them each night and collected each morning. That way we don't have as many health problems. They welcome the idea of exercise, when they're allowed."

Hobart Townes's voice trembled slightly—Hackler imagined from the unaccustomed cold—as he asked, "You use the same techniques with the female prisoners, too, then?"

"Yes, sir. And we've discovered that when we allow the male prisoners to see the female prisoners, it has a solid effect because the males know the females are being treated the same way and when we get any unruliness among the males or females, we make it clear that what happens to one group as punishment will be meted out to the other. Two nights ago a half dozen of the male prisoners tried to get out of the pit and assault the guard station. Two Special Forces officers, a Navy SEAL, a Marine, and two Air Police. They never made it, but we punished everyone—male and female—the next night, by hosing everyone down, halving rations, and only distributing half as many blankets."

"What about the six men?"

"They could prove useful to the project you mentioned on the phone, so rather than permanently damaging them we put them in the cold room. They were to be released this morning, but I thought you'd like to see the effect; so we held them over."

"Excellent." Townes nodded. "So far, I must admit, I'm not only impressed with the defensive readiness of Fort Makowski, but your handling of the detention aspect here as well. It should prove ideal for our purposes."

Hackler, after spending precious little time with Hobart Townes, still knew better than to ask for specifics. He gestured for Townes to continue their walking tour of the detention facility, Townes starting ahead again, burrowing deeper into the upturned collar of his coat. . . .

David Holden stood beside the tables on which the radios were set. He smoked a cigarette.

"This Bob Twobears is a straight guy," Mitch Diamond said. "We've dealt with his cell before for acquisition of intelligence and in some Canadian stuff, with them so close to the border and all. He calls himself a war chief."

"That's different from calling himself a colonel, isn't it?" Holden remarked, looking not at Diamond but at Rosie. She was sitting in the corner of the communications tent, her black field jacket wide open, a pink sweater glaringly bright beneath it. "What gave him the idea of contacting us?"

"The message didn't go into a hell of a lot of detail, David. But, I guess they figured we had more experience."

Patsi Alfredi spoke. "Some of our guys go to Montana and hit this fortress and bust out all these Army officers?"

"All different service branches," Rosie interjected.

"And there's no information on the plan, of course," Holden barely whispered.

"None. Just asking if we can come," Mitch Diamond responded.

Holden looked at the glowing tip of his cigarette. He was smoking too much. He stubbed out the cigarette in the ashtray on the corner of the nearest table. "Do what you can to get some more specifics. What kind of base, how many prisoners. I don't want us initiating force against the regular military yet, unless it's absolutely necessary. We'd be burning valuable bridges we might need to cross someday. Find out all you can. Tell this Twobears gentleman that we're sympathetic, but we need more data in order to arrive at a decision." Holden turned around and looked at Mitch. "How fast?"

"Maybe a coupla hours if everybody in the telephone chain is around and we don't bump into equipment failures."

In recent days there had been periodic short-duration communications blackouts across entire sections of the country, either wildcat strikes by communications workers or something initiated by the Makowski government. No one had complete enough information yet to know which. "All right. We'll table this Montana matter pending further input. Meanwhile, that weapons shipment from Florida's still running overdue. Any word there, Mitch? Patsy?"

"The Martine girl's last CB transmission put her about fifty miles east of Metro and rollin'. She coulda bumped into some other roadblocks we didn't know about and been forced to go around. I don't know," Mitch Diamond concluded.

Patsy Alfredi added, "I haven't picked up anything strange."

"We could backtrack her route?" Rosie Shepherd suggested.

"Agreed," said Holden. "Rosie—get us about six people. We'll leave in about ten minutes. Soft clothes, fake ID and weapons stashed. Two vehicles. You and I'll take one ourselves."

Rosie nodded, then stood, zipping her coat.

Mitch Diamond said, "I'll get to work on the radio with Patsy, here—find out if something's up."

"You let Patsy do that, Mitch. Get going on this Bob Twobears deal and get us some facts. If we do wind up injecting ourselves into this situation, from the preliminaries it sounds as if we'll have to do it pretty quickly."

David Holden started to light another cigarette, told himself no, walked out of the tent. . . .

He knelt on one knee in the snow, forming another large snowball, placing it carefully amid the array of mounds already on the smoothed-out space before him, drew back a little, and studied it.

Smith heard the cabin door open. "What are you doing, Smith? Making a snowman?"

"Lilly, come here," he told her, without taking his eyes from the assorted lumps of snow of varying heights and shapes.

He heard the crunch of her boots in the snow behind him, felt her near him, looked at her as she gathered her skirts under her thighs and crouched down beside him. "This is the area around Widow's Table, isn't it? A model?"

"That's right."

Smith gestured to the highest mound of snow. "This is the mesa, and it slopes all the way down past the far wall of the canyon here, and toward the town. But between Fort Devon and here, Widow's Table, there are these mountains. My estimate would be that somewhere in here there's an antiaircraft installation for interdicting an airborne assault against Fort Makowski."

"That's bad," Lilly Twobears observed as he looked at her.

Smith laughed, thumbing his hat up from his forehead and leaning close to her, kissing her lightly on the lips. "No! That's good. That's the only way we'll ever make it out of there alive, assuming we can make it in."

He looked at her hands. She had them clutched together and bundled half inside the fabric of her skirt. "Come inside with me. It's cold out here."

Smith stood, Lilly standing beside him. "Do you think this will work?"

"I'll let you know after we try it." And, his right arm curling around her waist, he started up the steps of the porch beside her.

Chapter Fourteen

THE WALKWAY ALONG the perimeter of the cold room was bathed in orange light from the heat lamps, which Hackler flicked on from a bank of switches on the wall beside the reinforced double doors. But the ambient temperature there on the walkway was still incredibly cold and the condensed moisture on the steel grating, frozen over and its surface almost instantly beginning to thaw under the heat lamps, made walking dangerously slick.

Hackler held to the handrail, trying to keep some semblance of his military bearing but determined that to fall would be worse. Townes unabashedly clung to the rail with both hands.

The sound of the water could be heard distinctly, the moaning of the six men only faintly. The water, originating from a tap, ice encrusted, came as a fine, mistlike spray on the air over the pit below them, relentlessly soaking the six men against the far wall, slumped in ice-coated clothing beneath the weight of their chains. "They have survived remarkably well. Our chief medical man, Captain Liggett, has been monitoring their vital signs and has come away quite impressed with their endurance. So, aside from the disciplinary aspects, we're getting some useful input on survival in extreme cold. It's almost as if they're willing themselves to stay with it. But I think we've taught them to behave themselves, Mr. Townes."

"I agree. Release five of them. Pick one to die. He'll remain here until he succumbs. Then return his body to the pit out there with his five friends. I want the rest of them, all the prisoners, to know what the price is they'll pay. I want their hatred, I want fear."

The men looked more dead than alive now, Hackler thought. And he realized at once that he pitied them and was looking very hard at Hobart Townes. He'd met vile men in his life, but none so vile as this. "If I may suggest, Mr. Townes, why don't you select which of them is to die?" He'd also learned, over the years, to cover himself when decisions had to be made that might have grave repercussions in the future.

Townes looked back at him almost equally hard, but not hard enough.

Then he pointed down toward the six. "The one with the blond hair over there on the left."

"Lieutenant Billings, the Marine. I'll see to it that the other five are transferred immediately."

"One of our intelligence agencies was experimenting with the drug I mentioned to you briefly when you were notified of my inspection tour. It has some peculiar qualities, basically accelerating the process that in the fifties was known as brainwashing. These five men will be ideal as the first experimental subjects. They're strong, yet they're nearly broken. Have them transferred to isolation cells. See to their physical condition. Anyone too ill is to be killed. Those others should be kept at a health-maintenance level only. Doctor Masterson, the man who accompanied me, will be in charge of this program. Consult with him for the details and fulfill any of his requests."

"Yes, sir."

"And let's get the hell out of here. I'm freezing my ass off."

Hackler looked at the five men who might live and the one who was bound to die. Somehow Billings, the young Marine officer, was probably the luckiest.

Chapter Fifteen

HE HEARD THE sounds of vehicles coming toward the house and was rolling out from beneath the sheet and quilt in the next instant, Lilly sitting bolt upright in bed beside him. "Smith?"

"I don't know what it is. Here." And Smith rolled open the fingers of Lilly's right hand, pressing the butt of the Beretta 92F into it. He stood up, pulling up the black twill pants over his bare behind. "Safety's on. Wait here."

Smith grabbed up the .25 from the nightstand, with upward thumb pressure checking the safety, then thrusting the little pistol into his belt. The metal of the pistol was cold against the flesh of his abdomen, and the wooden floor, once he stepped off the braided rug, was cold beneath his bare feet. Lilly's son, Wisdom, had bought him slippers for Christmas the previous year, but like most times when he got up in a hurry, there wasn't the time to locate them wherever they wound up beside the bed.

Through the open bedroom door into the cabin's great room, his knee still stiff, making him limp a little. His rifle rested behind a spring-loaded panel in the wall. He tapped the panel and it popped open like a small door. Smith reached inside, the Heckler & Koch coming into his hands. With the bare heel of his right foot he pushed the panel closed. A slight tug to the two magazines—one up the magazine well and the other clamped beside it ready to shift into position—and he crossed the room toward the front door, confident the primary magazine was seated.

Not a light on in the cabin except the grow-light for Lilly's plants, which diffused a soft purplish glow over the floor; Smith stood in otherwise total darkness beside one of the windows, looking out onto the yard.

He recognized the vehicles. One of them belonged to Lilly's brother, Bob, the other to Henry Blackdog.

Smith inhaled, felt the corners of his mouth turning down. He held his position, not trusting to the sight of the vehicles alone, waiting to see faces.

As Bob Twobears's four-wheel-drive pickup slowed to a stop, the driver's side door opened, and beneath the dome light he could recognize Bob's plain, open face.

Bob and Lilly were as unalike physically as it seemed possible for brother and sister to be. Lilly was classically beautiful, Bob bland as mush. Out of the second vehicle, a Ford Bronco, stepped Henry.

The two men were joined there in the snow by two other Indians whom Smith recognized as Patriot cell members.

Smith stepped away from the window, calling across the room, "Lilly. It's your brother."

"Bob?"

"Unless I'm mistaken, he's your only brother; and I should have known that no one else but Bob would drop by after midnight without hailing on the radio first. Silly me. He'll want coffee. He usually does."

But already Lilly was getting lights on and starting for the kitchen. She was swathed in a heavy, ankle-length blue robe and enormous fuzzy slippers that were made to resemble hairy, monstrous animal feet, another of Wisdom's gifts.

"I brought you a sweater."

Smith nodded, starting across the room for the sweater.

He'd let Bob knock before answering the door. Smith leaned his rifle—the chamber was still empty—into the corner by the kitchen counter, took the sweater, said, "Thank you, Lilly," and pulled it on over his head, careful of how he moved his left upper arm and careful of the bandage there. He shoved the sleeves of the black cotton pullover up past his elbows. He left the little .25 automatic right where he'd put it. Trust was one thing, foolishness another.

The anticipated knock came. "You hungry?"

"Bob will be," Smith told her. "How about a slice of that coffee cake?"

"Good idea."

Smith nodded. It was good coffee cake too.

As he crossed the room toward the door, another knock sounding, he considered something that from time to time crossed his mind: how impossibly stupid Lilly's former husband, totally unrelated by blood but coincidentally bearing the same surname, had to have been. To let a woman of Lilly's charm and grace slip away from him. "Idiot."

"What?" Lilly called from the kitchen.

"Nothing important." Smith was at the door. He opened it and caught Bob in midknock. "Gee, how nice to see you, Bob. Your CB radio's not working? Maybe it's something I could take a look at."

"No, no, ahh—my radio's fine."

"Come in, Bob, come in. You mean that the cabin radio's malfunctioning?"

"No, no, ahh—I don't think so."

Bob, Henry, and the other two men were inside now. No one thought to close the door, so Smith reached past them and did, a little devil of blowing snow dying abruptly on the floor.

"Hi, Lilly!" Bob sang out across the room. The other men grunted their greetings.

Lilly gave them a wave as she disappeared into the bedroom. Smith and the four men reached the chairs surrounding the hearth, and Smith sat down in his easy chair, saying, "Gentlemen. Nice of you to stop by. Lilly and I were both troubled by insomnia this evening. You couldn't have arrived at a more propitious time."

"I'm sorry, all right?" Bob Twobears said emphatically.

As Smith started to respond, Lilly reappeared, carrying the slippers Wisdom had given him. "I've got coffee brewing and I'm warming up some coffee cake. Anyone wants anything else, tell me." Before Smith could take the slippers from her, she dropped to her knees by his chair, putting the slippers on his feet. "Would you like a cigar, Smith?"

"No, thank you, Lilly." She was up, moving off toward the kitchen again. Indeed, Smith thought, her former husband had plumbed new depths of stupidity.

"Smith," Henry began, "we've been in contact with the Metro Patriot Cell. They need specifics of a plan, what's involved. But they're considering—"

"Can you transmit the plan without compromising it?"

"I can't—"

"—guarantee it," Smith finished for Henry. "But that's the only way we'll get them, correct?"

"Right." Bob nodded somberly.

Smith could smell the coffee. "All right. We'll risk it." Bob was almost a brother-in-law, Henry was a good friend, and the other two men—Charlie and Rod—were longstanding acquaintances. And, in a way, he felt bad about lying to them. But it was for a good cause. "Here's the plan," Smith began.

Chapter Sixteen

RAIN POURED DOWN so heavily that, at times, Rose Shepherd was almost tempted to ask David Holden to pull off to the side of the road. And the darkness only made it worse, like an interminable, lightless tunnel seen through smudged glass. But even if she hadn't liked Kelly Martine as a person, the woman was a fellow Patriot and was, judging from the CB transmission Rosie was hearing now, in trouble.

So Rose Shepherd said nothing, only clutched her hands together a little more tightly and was glad for the seat belt she wore.

". . . that's a big Ten-Four on that roadblock buster, Sling-Man, headin' y'all's way on sixty mebbe five miles south o' y'all's Ten-Twenty. Bears on his tail, but they ain't no bears in the air, like 'cause the weather. This is Secret Sam sayin' so long, y'all."

"Sling-Man" was the CB handle David had acquired, the Biblical David a "sling-man" because of the weapon he'd used to fell Goliath. Her David—David Holden—was fighting an enemy even more deadly, a usurper President named Roman Makowski and an organization of lethally violent revolutionaries known as the Front for the Liberation of North America. "Thanks, Secret Sam. This is Sling-Man signing off." David threw the CB microphone onto the seat between them. There was a bill currently before the Congress sponsored by the Makowski administration to make the use of a mobile CB transmitter/receiver illegal for the duration of the "emergency" and to take any such units not already purchased off dealer shelves. But, for the moment at least, openly displaying a citizens band radio didn't invite an automatic pull-over by the police. "God, we're getting spread thin, Rosie," David said softly as he reached to the radio and adjusted the squelch.

"This isn't the time or place for it," Rose Shepherd told him as she started to climb over the front-seat back to get access to their weapons, "but this Montana thing sounds important; and if we don't do something, even something symbolic, against the PSF unit that's closed up Metro, we'll lose the confidence of the people." She generally enjoyed her sex, had never once regretted being a woman; but sometimes what was expected of women was a royal pain. David, so he'd look respectable, wore a sport coat and good slacks and shoes (plus a fake mustache and wash-out hair dye to change his appearance). She, on the other hand, wore a dress (not the easiest thing to wear crawling through a ditch with an M-16), the skirt of which shot up to her hips as she rolled over into the backseat. She extracted the small, single-cell Mag Lite from the pocket of her dress, twisted the head to turn it on, then clamped it between her teeth as she started working on the panel built into the fake drive-shaft hump, pulling the carpeting and padding away first.

"I know what you mean; that's what I meant about being spread too thin. If the information from that Indian Patriot cell is accurate, we have no choice but to do something. And you're right about reacting to the Metro thing too."

Mitch Diamond—she was glad Mitch had nothing worse to show for driving that explosives-laden truck than a few minor cuts—was a genius with cars, trucks, anything that rolled on four or more wheels. Lately, he was taking as many GM cars as he could get the parts for and converting them from rear-wheel drive to front-wheel drive, leaving the drive-shaft humps as the perfect storage areas for weapons and other items. So far, not a one of the few cars he had completed had been blown during a roadblock search. What he did, as far as she understood it, was to place rear-wheel-drive bodies on front-wheel-drive frames. She was sure it wasn't as simple as it sounded, but Mitch was Mitch and that seemed to say it all.

She was starting to open the drive-shaft hump, listening as David talked with Luther Steel on a CB sideband. Luther was driving the second car. ". . . so, obviously we don't want to shoot at police. But we can't let that truck Kelly's driving be intercepted either. We need what she's carrying. If we're lucky—I should bite my tongue—they won't be cops, but PSF."

She could hear Luther's voice coming back. "You've got an odd idea of luck."

"Let's play it by ear; if they're safe to hit, we use the open-ended Delta play. You're car's the one set up. If they aren't, I don't know."

Luther agreed.

She made it that they had about two minutes until engagement. Already she could faintly hear the sound of sirens in the distance.

One thing she had always liked about David was that he wasn't one of those men who was into fakey macho. If he didn't have the answer, he admitted it. And if he did, he didn't cram his answer down people's throats.

She began unlimbering the guns from the compartment inside and on both sides of the driveshaft hump. Two M-16's, the Uzi semiautomatic carbine, one of David's Berettas. Following the driveshaft hump beneath the rear seat still further, she extracted her Glock-17, David's knife and her own knife, and the spare magazines for the guns. The floor between the front- and backseats was almost completely torn up.

"David! Hot!" Rose Shepherd said indistinctly, through clenched teeth still clamped around the small flashlight.

David reached back and she gently set the full-sized Beretta 92F into his right palm.

"Knife."

He reached back again and took the Defender knife, its sheath detached from the offside magazine pouches of his shoulder holster, where he usually carried it.

"Magazines."

He reached back and she gave him the four spare magazines she'd packed for him, putting them into his hand two at a time.

"I've got an M-16 and four magazines for you."

"Right. We'll be on them in under a minute. I can see Mars lights in the distance, coming from around the bend in the road."

She looked up, extinguishing the small flashlight she'd used for light to work by, dropping it back into the pocket. Luther's car was coming up alongside them now. She slung her purse cross body like a musette bag, right shoulder to left hip, the Glock inside it, chamber empty. The Delta play David had discussed over the CB was their code phrase for a standard roadblocking technique, and recognizable even to the most inexperienced law-enforcement personnel. Both cars would form a wedge, noses forward, making the road impassable to anything short of a tank, all but suicidal to smash through with vehicles the size of the vans used by the PSF.

If possible they'd use the maneuver to separate the truck driven by Kelly Martine—an eighteen-wheeler marked as belonging to one of the fast-food chains—from the pursuit vehicles. Once the pursuit vehicles were stopped, Luther Steel would activate explosives already set in the car he drove, Steel, Runningdeer, LeFleur, and Blumenthal joining David and her. When the explosives detonated, the flaming car would block the road by itself.

It would be the first time they'd ever tried this.

"Hang on, Rosie. We're here."

She licked her lips, wishing there were time for lipstick because her lips felt dry and chapped.

Instead, she chamber-loaded her M-16.

Chapter Seventeen

THE SEMI WAS riding the double yellow lines at the center of the four lanes of rain-glistening highway. Holden had the CB radio set to Channel 19. "Kelly. If you read me, come back. This is David Holden. Over."

"Thank God! Where are you?"

Her transmission was crystal clear. They were little more than a city block's distance apart. "Give it all the speed you can safely make and cut between us. I'm in the car on your right and this car will be coming up after you. I'm blinking my headlights now. Copy that?"

"I see you! Hang on!"

"Patriot vehicle two, execute Delta. I repeat. Execute Delta, now. Confirm."

"Executing Delta."

Holden glanced right. Steel's car was veering off toward the far shoulder as Holden cut the wheel sharply to the left, toward the opposite shoulder. He caught a glimpse of Rosie in his rearview, her M-16 bisecting her body in a high port.

The eighteen-wheeler was coming fast, a wake of spray from the standing water through which it cut rising on either side of it. Holden's windshield wipers were already at full speed, and as the truck sped past, Holden's field of vision was momentarily obscured in the wave of spray. The car was starting to hydroplane, Holden fighting the wheel, still less familiar than he should have been with front-wheel-drive maneuvering. But he held it.

After the truck had barreled past, at the first glimpse of the road when the spray cleared, Holden cut the wheel right.

Three vans bearing the markings of the Presidential Strike Force, blue Mars lights flashing, were closing fast, about two hundred yards behind the eighteen-wheeler. "Out!" Holden shouted as he stomped the brake and the car skidded diagonally, almost fully blocking the two on-coming lanes.

As Holden slid across the seat and out the passenger door, he could see Steel's car, grinding to a stop in a spray of water, blocking the other two lanes. Runningdeer, LeFleur, and Blumenthal were already out of the car, Blumenthal bringing up the Hawk MM-1 grenade launcher as Steel rolled out from behind the wheel.

Rosie was opening fire.

As Holden ducked down beside her, she pushed the sec-ond M-16 toward him. Holden caught it in midair with his left hand at the front stock, his right hand racking the bolt. As he cheeked the rifle, he thumbed the selector to auto and fired for the windshield of the lead van.

In the same instant, Blumenthal's grenade launcher lob-bed its first round, the road surface between two of the vans exploding, one of the vans swerving, trying to stop, skid-ding, flipping onto its side on the rain-slicked pavement, sliding across the road toward them in a shower of sparks.

The windshield of the first van was blown out, Holden crediting the hit to himself or Rosie. There was no time to worry about it more than that as he swung the rifle toward the overturned van. It was coming right toward Steel's car, which was loaded with enough explosives to crater out the roadbed.

Holden fired out the thirty-round magazine in the M-16.

The van still skidded toward them, a man trying to climb out the passenger door, falling, crushed beneath the weight of the van.

"Run for it! Randy—we'll use the grenade launcher if we need to; don't—" The screeching of steel across pavement was too loud now, but Steel and the three ex-FBI men were already running, spraying out M-16's toward the third van as they ran.

Holden threw the empty M-16 into the backseat of the car and launched himself across the front seat to drop behind the wheel, Rosie firing out her M-16.

Holden stomped the brake and threw into reverse, shouting, "Rosie!"

As Steel and his three men crowded into the rear seat, Rosie jumped in front beside him, her door still open as Holden stomped the accelerator, cutting the wheel so sharply, he almost made the car overturn, stomping the brake pedal, throwing the car into drive.

The PSF van impacted Steel's car as Holden cut the wheel hard right, swerving all over the road as he fought to hold the steering, in the rearview mirror a flash of intense yellow light, in the next instant a roar that sounded like some stupendous wave crashing down. "Look out!" Steel shouted.

Something hit the rear of the car, Holden fighting the steering again, at last getting it under control and accelerating away.

In the sideview mirror he could see the mushroom-shaped fireball, orange and yellow, roaring upward into the rain-soaked darkness.

And, swerving past it, a solitary set of blue Mars lights.

Runningdeer climbed over into the front seat, between Holden and Rosie.

Steel's driver's-side rear window was down and he was firing his pistol.

Like red eyes staring out of the darkness, Holden could just make out the taillights of Kelly Martine's truck well along down the road. Gradually, he pressed the accelerator closer to the floor, the Chevy's interceptorlike engine roaring now.

The fireball behind them was dying, the blue light bar blindingly intense now as the PSF van pursued. "Keep her steady!" Rosie shrieked, her window down, the semiauto Uzi carbine in her left fist, her right hand closed over the top of the barrel and front handguard as she fired.

Rain drove through the open window with near blinding intensity now, Holden's eyes squinted against it as he drove. Hot brass from Rosie's weapon sprayed across the front seat, Runningdeer hissing, "God bless it!"

Holden was gaining on the truck, but the van was keeping the same distance back, neither gaining nor falling off. Holden flattened the pedal full to the floor, both fists locked white-knuckled on the steering wheel, the wind-driven rain seeming to tear across the highway now with greater ferocity than before, the windshield wipers, at full speed, barely noticeable in their effect.

"Blumenthal! Fire the grenade launcher if you can!"

"Yes, sir!"

Holden shot a quick glance right, Rosie still firing the Uzi semi. "Rosie—pull back!"

The window on the passenger side squeaked as Blumenthal lowered it, Blumenthal telling LeFleur, "Tom! Hold my belt! I gotta lean out far."

There was a shaft of diffused yellow light from the top of the van, and Holden knew its origin. The PSF vans were equipped with moon-roof panels that could be drawn back so a man could stand up and fire from inside the vehicle.

In the next instant, assault-rifle fire stitched across the side of the car, Holden hearing the ricochets as they whined off. "Look out!" Another burst of assault-rifle fire.

"The wind—" Steel started to yell, but the rear windshield blew inward, cutting him off.

Rosie screamed, "Stay down!"

The boom of Blumenthal's grenade launcher.

A yellow-and-white fireball belched upward into the darkness. The pursuing PSF van swerved, punching through the edge of the fireball. But it kept coming. Another burst of assault-rifle fire, Holden ducking down, the back of his neck already feeling the bite of slivered glass.

The grenade launcher fired again, then again, bracketing the van. The van seemed to jump as Holden—almost unable to separate his gaze from it—stared into the rearview.

The grenade launcher fired again, catching the van.

The PSF pursuit vehicle seemed to hesitate in the air for a split second, and then it was gone, engulfed in fire and smoke.

Holden could hear Rosie's voice on the CB, saying, "Kelly. This is Rosie. Slow her down. We nailed the guys. Copy that?"

"I copy. Come up alongside."

David Holden tried easing his grip on the steering wheel. His fingers were so rigid, they could barely move.

Chapter Eighteen

IN THE DARKNESS beside Smith, Lilly's voice was barely a whisper as she asked, "Why didn't you tell them your plan the way you told it to me?"

Bob and Henry were sleeping in Wisdom's room, the other men who had accompanied them on the sofa and in an easy chair by the fire. Lilly had promised to awaken them just before dawn so they could drive down the mountain and reestablish contact with the Metro Patriot Cell.

Matthew Smith stared up at the ceiling for a time, not answering her, just listening to the pleasant sound of her breathing, holding her left hand in his right beneath the covers. "When a secret is shared, Lilly, it's no longer a secret. I presented them with the correct outlines of the plan. What I deleted was how the supposed antiaircraft positions figure in. To have relied on something about the existence of which I'm only guessing in the first place would be dangerously presumptuous at any event. And, if you're not tired, that's fine. But you're awakening me before you awaken them, remember?"

And Smith turned over onto his right side, propping himself on his elbow, resting his right cheek against the knuckles of his fist. "You are very beautiful and very intelligent. And one of your most charming features is that you so little realize, Lilly, how rare those qualities are, especially combined in one person."

Her fingers touched at his cheek and Smith took her face in his left hand, his right arm going behind her, drawing her up to him. "And I love you, Lilly, more than I have ever loved before or could ever love again."

Smith kissed her hard on the mouth as her body molded against his. . . .

"Listen to the Exhortation of the Dawn!
    Look to this Day!
For it is Life, the very Life of Life.
In its brief course lie all the Verities and Realities of your
        Existence:
    The Bliss of Growth,
    The Glory of Action,
    The Splendor of Beauty.
For Yesterday is but a Dream,
And Tomorrow is only a Vision;
But Today well lived makes every Yesterday a Dream of
        Happiness,
And every Tomorrow a Vision of Hope.
Look well therefore to this Day!
Such is the Salutation of the Dawn."

Araby tossed her pretty head, the black of her mane glistening wet; and, as he urged her ahead with his knees through the fresh drifted snow, he remarked to her, " 'The Salutation of the Dawn,' as doubtless you are aware owing to your desert heritage. Come on!" And Smith urged her forward again, the big chestnut mare attacking the drifts as if she were charging an enemy, leaping upon them, bursting through them, scattering them before her force and strength. Smith screwed his Stetson down lower over his eyes and squinted against the icy spray on the wind. It numbed the flesh of his face and he hunkered down more deeply into the collar of his coat.

Smith never gambled beyond the demands of necessity. Now was such a time. The prisoners at Fort Makowski—how vile to name anything after such a man as this usurper President—required rescuing, one way or the other, freeing them or killing them, in either case rescuing them from the fate they now endured. If, indeed, he found today what he expected he would find, what logic and experience and judgment demanded he would find, then there was a chance, however slim, for success.

Without that chance he would be forced to violate every principle by which he had lived. Suicide—which a raid against Fort Makowski would indeed be without the presence of the antiaircraft installations—was the abdication of self, and something he viewed as morally wrong, although his option because he owned his life and it was his to do with as he desired and was able.

Dawn peeked timidly out from beneath the horizon line, pale yellow under a heavy quilt of gray so bleak it was almost black. In an hour or so Araby's exertion from the ride under these extreme conditions would necessitate rest; then, after another hour, he would be so close to the summit of the mountain that it would be necessary to continue the climb on foot. Araby's reins in his left hand, Smith rubbed at his right knee.

Atop the summit he would find nothing or he would find what he sought, death irreconcilable or a ray of hope weaker than the light that struggled to emerge into morning.

It was the first time he'd ever tried anything from the Sanskrit with Araby. She usually responded best to Shakespeare or Milton.

Chapter Nineteen

BILL RUNNINGDEER PRIED open the top of the crate and Rosie Shepherd began to remove the packing pads and sheets of desiccant.

Kelly Martine stood beside Holden; she was drinking a cup of coffee from a large white ceramic mug of the kind sometimes found in truck stops. "Hope you guys like this shit," she remarked. "Pure hell gettin' it here."

David Holden took a single step forward and reached into the case, his right hand closing over the receiver—still greasy with Cosmoline—of the 7.62mm G-3.

"With these," Holden began, taking the Heckler & Koch assault rifle from the case, "and the other weapons you've brought, we have equal or better firepower than the Presidential Strike Force. We can arm a special unit within the cell, and we can hit a very special place." He meant the underground facility to which Luther Steel had introduced Rosie and himself, a place where there were rooms whose walls were lined with the weapons needed to help in deposing the tyrant Makowski, ridding the country of the FLNA, restoring freedom to the land.

He looked at Rosie. She was smiling at him strangely, as if somehow she knew his thoughts. She walked over to stand beside him, but first leaned up and kissed him lightly on the mouth and whispered, "I love you."

David Holden replaced the rifle in its case with the others. There were more cases of G-3's, cases of MP-5 sub-machine guns, ammunition, magazines, spare parts.

Holden reached toward Rosie Shepherd's face, and only then remembered the grease on his hand. . . .

Mitch Diamond entered the command tent, Holden looking up from the Metro street map he had been study-ing. Possibilities for doing something substantial against the PSF occupation forces in Metro didn't look that good. He hadn't slept, too fired by adrenaline from the fight on the highway. "You hear from them?"

"Bob Twobears came back with this." He held up a note-pad.

Rosie said, "Read it, Mitch."

Mitch Diamond shrugged his massive shoulders, scratched at the skin of his left cheek near the bandage there, then said, "I didn't copy it down word for word or anything." He looked down at the pad in his hands, re-minding Holden somehow of a schoolboy beginning a reci-tation. "They're working with a man who isn't a member of the cell, but they say he's really good. He came up with the plan. They say they plan to steal a train and penetrate the fort, then rescue the prisoners, get 'em aboard the train, and use the train to get them out. They say we need PSF uniforms for all our people—they can get their own—and there are some other details but they don't want to lay it all out yet. We steal the train when it slows down somewhere between the town of Fort Devon and this piss-assed Fort Makowski. Fort Makowski is a big collection of block-houses with a really 'substantial'—that's their word—wall around it. They don't really know where the prisoners are being kept, in which building, ya know. And they don't know how many prisoners there are. But they figure a good number of them would be able to fight."

"What about the road—there's gotta be a road, right?" Rosie asked.

David Holden looked at her and smiled. "And what about aircraft? Any mention of that?"

Mitch Diamond answered, "I got it written down here that they know there are a lot of details they aren't going into, but they have 'em all covered. At least, this Smith guy does."

"Smith?" Rosie asked, echoing Holden's own thoughts.

"Smith. That's the guy they say came up with the plan and knows what he's doin'."

David Holden lit a cigarette. He realized how a war might be instantly won: cut off the supply of cigarettes to the enemy. "I'm glad somebody does."

"What?" Mitch asked.

"Knows what he's doing."

Holden exhaled and watched the smoke for a second, then turned to the United States map on the tent wall and started looking at northwestern Montana for a place called Fort Devon.

Chapter Twenty

HIS RIFLE WAS still on the saddle. He'd reasoned that he needed two hands for climbing, and if he should fall—because the approach to the summit was at once steep and slick—a rifle would only make it easier to break his back.

His knee no longer bothered him, hadn't after the first few minutes of the walk. But the strain of the climb was beginning to tell on his left upper arm and he thought he might be bleeding through. Or it might only be sweat.

The rock chimney through which he moved now was black and wet, and with great care he would move one foot, then a hand, then the other foot, then the other hand. He was already more than a dozen feet up the chimney and a fall here could prove fatal, either immediately or as a result of incapacitating injury.

Matthew Smith kept going upward, the gloved fingers of his right hand at last curling over the ledge above. He stayed there a moment, catching his breath, organizing his thoughts. The availability of aerial reconnaissance would have obviated any need for his present endeavor; but only the enemy had that capability now. He grunted once, shook his head, set his jaw, and climbed up out of the chimney, rolling over onto the snow of the ledge.

Smith looked down. The chimney below was dizzyingly steep. He looked across the valley beyond the edge of the ledge.

Snowcapped mountaintops surrounded the valley in all directions, patches of darker gray within the overcast somehow seeming to redirect the sunlight, making the white of the peaks glisten with a surreal brightness. The stream below sparkled crystal clear, and as he stood up and inhaled, the air, albeit cold, was tinglingly fresh in his lungs and nostrils.

When he'd left the United States Marshals Service, one of the women he'd worked with had asked him, "Why are you moving to the middle of nowhere, Smith?"

He smiled as he remembered her, very dark brown eyes in a face the color of which reminded him of expensive milk chocolate. And she was a good cop as well. He'd told her, "Mary Ann, don't you ever get tired of looking at concrete?"

There was puzzlement in those pretty eyes. "Concrete?"

"Cement walls and paving squares in sidewalks."

"I don't understand, Smith."

"Try this, Mary Ann: air that smells like air instead of emissions. Have you ever smelled real air?"

"Like when we were stuck out by that lake for two weeks on that witness protection job?"

"Yes. Exactly that, only better."

"But there wasn't anyone else around, nothin' but trees and sky and birds and stuff!"

He'd put his hands to her shoulders, looked her square in the eye, said, "Exactly!" and kissed her on the forehead.

Smith shook his head. Mary Ann would have hated it here. He hunched his shoulders and burrowed his neck deeper into his collar. His right hand opened the flap of the El Paso 1940 holster at his right hip and he drew the Beretta, wiping off the safety with his thumb.

If he met someone unexpectedly he wanted to be prepared with a proper greeting.

Chapter Twenty-One

SLOPPY JOES. FOR a change there was an abundance of fresh hamburger buns and ground beef at the same time. Rose Shepherd, like most of the Patriots, helped out the women who ran the kitchen whenever she could. And stirring huge frying pans of browning ground beef hadn't been that much of a challenge, for her modest culinary skills, at any rate. With two sandwiches on her plate and a mound of french fries, and a second plate identical to the first, only mounded higher with fries and the mixture of beef and sauce—for David—she started across the compound, careful of the uneven ground lest she spill the contents from the iced tea glasses set into the circular compartments at the centers of each plate.

She saw David sitting on a camp stool beside the stream that flowed along the edge of the compound and hailed him. He looked her way, smiled and waved, and she walked toward him. He stood up as she approached, taking the fuller of the two plates she offered him. "I thought you'd be hungry."

He smiled. "Yeah, I guess I am."

He cocked his head toward the camp stool, but she told him, "No—you take it. I'm just as comfortable on my knees. But you can hold my plate for a second."

David took the second plate and sat down as she dropped to her knees beside the camp stool, then took back her plate. She had a sip of the iced tea, then looked around for a level spot of ground on which to set the plastic glass. "Here," David said, taking the glass from her, setting it on the ground beside his.

"I've got forks," Rose volunteered, reaching into the left breast pocket of her black BDU blouse, handing David one, keeping the other for herself.

He was chewing on a french fry as he told her, "I think I've got it figured out—maybe."

"How we're gonna be two places at once?"

"Logic dictates that we do both jobs at once, Rosie; you take one and I take one." Her heart sank, although she knew his decision was the only realistic option and had been waiting for him to announce it. "One of us does the job in Montana and one of us hits the underground facility to clean out all the weapons and everything else there we can use. Then the combined forces hit the PSF in Metro. Which do you want?"

She looked at him, then down at her food—it was getting cold—and back into his eyes. They were pretty eyes, she'd always thought. And she could see the love in them for her when sadness hadn't crowded it out sometimes. "Whichever one you think is best, David." She knew which was the most dangerous, and that was the one in Montana. The job at the underground facility could be aborted if the odds looked too great, and might well prove to be nothing more than a clandestine penetration and a fast but arduous clean-out of the place for anything useful.

"Why don't you set up the job here, and I'll take the job in Montana. I'll bring Luther and Bill with me and a few more guys. That'll leave you Tom and Randy and everybody else, and Mitch can organize the rolling stock you'll need."

"All right. When are you leaving?"

"Tonight," he told her softly, looking down at his food.

She'd been set up for the safer of the two missions, but she respected him for making it that obvious and at least giving her a choice. "But one thing," Rose said to him.

"Yeah?"

"We make love before you go. All right?"

He stopped eating, the fork poised before his mouth. "I was thinking the same thing," David told her.

"Good." She nodded, swallowing hard even though there wasn't anything in her mouth.

Chapter Twenty-Two

IN THE BOOK she was reading, the heroine was desperately in love with the hero, saw him as her ideal. Lilly Twobears set down her book, looked at the clock on the mantelpiece.

Matthew would be on the mountain now, his reconnaissance well under way. And she was terrified for him. And for herself. It was as if Matthew Smith had freed her from slavery, the worst kind, that which was self-imposed. Should he die, she would die; her death would not be the physical kind, because there was her son Wisdom to think about. It would be the other kind, where someone withered inside slowly and there was never any happiness.

Matthew had given her dignity, not restored it, because something could not be restored that had never before existed. He had given her happiness. And then this stupid war came along. First the Front for the Liberation of North America had begun to destroy the very fabric of life in the United States. An evil impulse had seized her for a split second, at first, when she'd realized what was happening: Let the white man feel what it was like to have his country invaded, his people murdered and violated, his homelands ravished.

But two wrongs, as they say, did not make a right; and the Indian would never be restored, despite all the Matthew Smiths of the world could do— And she smiled. Matthew, perhaps, could do it. He was a man of incredible proportions, the embodiment of the very word.

She was staring through the window, into the freshly falling snow.

"Come home," she whispered.

And then he would leave again, whether this commando raid against Fort Makowski took place with the help of the Metro Patriots or not. He would not let these helpless prisoners languish there to die.

A smile crossed her lips as a thought crossed her mind. However beautiful Matthew's black-maned chestnut mare Araby was, he needed a horse of gleaming white.

Chapter Twenty-Three

AT THE SUMMIT, the ledge behind him, waiting for his return like an enemy who had tried and failed and would try again—the rock was slippery, uneven, the width of the ledge impossibly narrow at times—he watched through his binoculars.

There was the chimney to be reckoned with again. It was almost invariably more difficult to climb down than up.

Through the binoculars he saw what he had come to see, and the realization of that warmed him.

A dome-shaped structure, a satellite dish, a radar antenna, an obvious gun emplacement, all neatly camouflaged in white—and the falling snow only enhanced the effect.

"Don't move, motherfucker!"

Matthew Smith closed his eyes, temporarily lowering the glasses. There had been no trail sign to indicate the presence of a man on the summit here. This meant that the man and whoever might be with him had come the long way from the far side of the mountain, likely part of the small garrison at the town of Fort Devon. "If I didn't move, we would both be here until doomsday, wouldn't we? And as to the reference to my mother, you've obviously never heard of the 'The Knight's Toast,' an unparalleled paean to motherhood."

"Shut up, man. And get up nice and slow."

"You've obviously never heard of adverbs either."

Slowly, Smith turned around on his back, eyeing the PSF trooper, the man's M-16 assault rifle pointed at Smith's chest. Only one man was visible, which meant his comrades, if any, were below the summit. The man's snow goggles were down and he held the rifle like a length of two-by-four. "I'll unbuckle my gun belt," Smith volunteered, standing up.

The trooper took a half step forward.

If Smith killed the man with the little .25 submerged below his waistband, the other PSF personnel would be here instantly.

As Smith moved his left hand to the two-piece brass buckle, his right hand, full of snow, snapped forward, hurling the snow into the PSFer's eyes and face, Smith's left hand grasping at the muzzle of the rifle as he pivoted on the ball of his left foot, getting his own body plane behind the muzzle of the M-16.

Smith's left thumb flicked the Colt assault rifle's safety tumbler from auto to safe as his right hand, the Beretta drawn from the tied-down flap holster at his hip, crashed downward, across the back of the PSFer's skull and onto the neck. There was a crack that sounded as loud as a small-caliber pistol shot, but wouldn't carry as a shot would.

The man's body trembled, eyes wide open. Smith had broken the Presidential Strike Force trooper's neck and the man was already dead as the husk of what he had been tumbled forward into the snow at Smith's feet.

Smith bent over the body, shook his head, and sighed. The PSFer was hardly past his mid-twenties, likely younger. "Just a boy."

Smith stood up.

He started along the trail down from the summit, backtracking the dead man, searching for anything that might indicate a second set of footprints in the snow. But the only sign Smith found showed clearly just one man, meaning the others were still well back, perhaps had not yet reached the chimney, which was Smith's only way down the mountain without walking it out and certainly bumping right into them.

But whoever else had been with this hapless fellow would be coming up to the summit quickly enough.

Smith backtracked himself now, dropping to one knee beside the body of the PSF trooper. Smith holstered his weapon.

He searched the dead man for any papers, but found only military ID and both a military driver's license and a civilian license, the latter issued by the state of Ohio.

One could sometimes determine a good deal from a dead man by his belongings. Such was not the case here. Emergency field rations only, which meant this was a routine, short-range patrol. There was nothing else of real consequence.

"Rest in peace," Smith murmured, thumbing down the dead man's eyes. They would open again; but by that time the body would be somewhere near the base of the mountain. Smith took up the man's M-16, slung it crossbody to the man's back, then hauled the body up, throwing his left shoulder into the dead man's midsection and hauling him up into a fireman's carry. The trooper was heavier than he looked.

Slowly, because of the added weight, Smith started toward the ledge. There were enough spots there where the footing was tricky that it would appear convincing that this man had merely fallen and broken his neck rather than been deliberately killed. The cold weather would be a worthwhile ally in this endeavor, frustrating the autopsy should one be performed.

Then it would be back to the summit, erase as well as possible the signs of what had taken place—the fresh snow now falling would help that—and then make for the rock chimney. With any luck he'd make it before the other PSF personnel showed up.

Smith quickened his pace as best he could.

Chapter Twenty-Four

"LINDA? JUST ME." He could hear the shower running as he entered the suite of rooms he and Linda Effingham shared under Dimitri Borsoi's beach-house roof.

Kearney closed the door behind him, still sweating from his postponed and rescheduled "morning run." He was perspiring despite the unseasonably cool weather along the beachfront, a message from his body that he'd needed the run, that the forced inactivity of "hanging around" with Borsoi and Montenegro, as he tried to ingratiate himself with the organization, was beginning to tell. But he was satisfied that he'd run well.

The run was scrubbed for the morning hours when Borsoi and Montenegro had asked him to accompany them. Kearney could not refuse the offer. His assignment, as it had been given to him, was in reach—find the head of the Front for the Liberation of North America and assassinate him. Implicit in the orders he'd received that day in London was that he should also do as much damage to the FLNA's infrastructure as possible.

It was under this rather fuzzy guideline that he still labored. He could kill Dimitri Borsoi, alias "Mr. Johnson," at any time. None of Borsoi's street-punk bodyguards posed that serious a threat unless he—Kearney—should proceed carelessly.

Yet the idea that Borsoi might not be the top man still

nagged, and Ricardo Montenegro, the drug kingpin and Borsoi's apparent equal, intrigued him.

And the proposition.

The ramifications of that concept were the most intriguing of all.

They wanted to build him into a media-star leader for the FLNA.

He shivered, telling himself it was the perspiration drying.

The shower was still running. Geoffrey Kearney shook his head, threw his towel down at the foot of the bed, sat down beside it, and and then stood up again to take a cigarette and his brass Zippo lighter from the nightstand on his side of the bed.

"Don't hurry, darling!" Kearney called out to Linda, but she evidently didn't hear him.

He stuck the tip of the cigarette into the flame of the lighter and inhaled. He'd gotten his cigarette smoking under control again, to less than a pack a day. Control had gone out the window for a while there.

"Linda?"

She still didn't answer.

There was no sin in having a weapon to hand here at Borsoi's home, so Geoffrey Kearney reached into the nightstand drawer, found the 5906, and checked it. It looked not to have been tampered with. The cigarette in the right corner of his mouth, the pistol in his right hand, Kearney started for the bathroom door. "Linda!"

He knocked on the door, but there was no answer. He tried the door. It opened easily.

As he opened the door, a cloud of steam rushed at him and there was water on the floor, the shower door halfway open.

Kearney crossed the bathroom and found Linda half sitting at the rear of the shower. "My God," he hissed. Had she slipped and struck her— The cigarette went into the toilet, the gun onto the vanity counter.

The water was hot. He was soaked reaching for her with one hand, killing the shower spray with the other, shutting off both faucets too.

He was half into the shower. "Linda?" There was no blood. There was a pulse, strong albeit a bit irregular. He gently felt along her body for any obvious fractures as her head lolled forward toward him and he caught her breath.

She reeked of alcohol. . . .

Wrapped in a terry cloth bathrobe, her hair wrapped in a towel—he wasn't good at making turbans—Linda, bedraggled looking, stared at him, her right hand shaking as she held her cigarette. Geoffrey Kearney was on his third since scooping her up out of the shower. "I need a drink."

"No, you don't."

"I'll be fine if I have a drink."

"No, you won't."

"I know if I'll be fine or not."

"So do I. Looks as though you won't be fine if it depends on a drink."

She started to stand up, then grabbed at her stomach, and he thought she was going to vomit again as he reached for the ice bucket he'd just rinsed out after the last time.

But she just slumped back into the chair instead.

"What's happening to you?" Kearney asked her, his voice low, as controlled as he could make it sound.

"I was tired, so I sat down. Is that a crime?"

"No. Most people don't sit down in the shower, so forgive my surprise. But why were you drinking so damned early in the day?"

"I wasn't wearing my damn watch." She wasn't laughing, not even smiling, just staring at him, a little glassy eyed still, her speech a little slurred. Geoffrey Kearney stood up and began methodically to search the room. "What are you looking for?"

"The bottle of whiskey on the dresser is still half full, just as it was last evening before we went to bed. I'm looking for the bottle of gin, because gin is what I smelled on your breath. If you want to disguise the fact you've been drinking, darling, try vodka next time. I believe in some circles in America vodka is called 'the teacher's drink' because you won't smell like you've been drinking.

"Better still, next time don't—" He caught the faintest whiff of odor and pulled down a suitcase from the shelf above the clothes pole in the closet. He threw the case on the bed and opened it, the smell stronger, the sound of glass tinkling. Two empty bottles, both quart sized, both gin. He looked at the labels in disgust. "This stuff—"

"It tasted good to me, Geoff."

Kearney put the bottles down and just looked at her. As if the men in London to whom he reported were whispering to him from inside his head, he could hear their words plainly. "You must kill her before she inadvertently blows your cover and gets you both killed."

Inside his head, so only they could hear, he said, *Fuck off*.

Chapter Twenty-Five

HE STOOPED AND entered the tent, the light from the gray late afternoon sky diffusing through the canvas, but no more than enough to cast the enclosure in a heavily textured gray.

Near the center of the tent he saw her as a brief flash of whiteness before the tent flap fell closed behind him.

He stood there, not wanting to close his eyes to hasten their adjustment to the poorer light, for fear of the loss of a split second of seeing her.

Gradually, David Holden could see Rosie Shepherd in greater clarity.

She knelt on a blanket spread over their air mattress, knees and thighs tight together, arms folded over her breasts, hands touching her shoulders. She was naked from the waist down, but wore some dark garment—maybe a black BDU blouse or one of his sweaters—above the waist.

It was a BDU blouse, because as he approached her and her arms unfolded toward him, the BDU blouse opened and he could see her breasts, whiter against the blackness of the garment.

Holden dropped to his knees before her, her arms entwining around his neck. "I love you, David."

"I know that." And he kissed her mouth very hard, her breasts pressed tight against his chest, her fingers moving in his hair. His fingers touched at Rosie's bare shoulders, then splayed back, the palms of his hands frictioning down along her arms, at last encountering the fabric of the BDU blouse, then continuing their downward movement, pulling it free of her body.

Her hands went to his waist, found the buckle of his trouser belt.

Holden shrugged out of the field jacket, then out of his shoulder holster as her hands opened his belt, then opened one at a time the buttons of his BDU pants.

He was already hard before she touched him and he shivered when her fingers pressed against him. He drew her close to him, kissing her again, harder than before, her hands exploring him as his explored her.

Holden brought her down with him onto the blanket, his fingers brushing over her nipples. They were hard.

Her body molded against his as Holden slipped between Rosie Shepherd's thighs.

Chapter Twenty-Six

CHESTER LITTLE'S CARGO plane stood, engines revving, at the end of the field.

David Holden stopped the car he was driving, letting the other cars go on ahead.

Rose never took her eyes off him. "If you get killed or something dumb like that," she told him, "I'm gonna really be pissed, and you know how I am when I'm angry."

David nodded, smiled, responding, "I'd be pretty upset myself, I think. And if you go getting killed or anything, well, you're in deep shit with me, Rosie."

She shrugged her shoulders and raised her eyebrows. "Well, looks like we'll both have to make it through, then, or we're both gonna be sore at each other."

"No argument there," David agreed.

"Why do you love me?" The words sort of spilled out of her, and she was sorry she'd asked the moment she heard herself say them.

"What?"

"No—forget it, I'm just glad that you do"—and she leaned across and hugged both her arms around his right arm, holding it over her between her breasts.

"No—you asked, fine," David said. She held on to him tighter than she'd ever held on to anything in her life. "There isn't any one reason or any ten reasons. I could give you a long list of the things I love about you, but that's not why I love you. I figure, if I could just say, 'I love you because of your eyes or your hair or the sound of your voice—"

"You could have mentioned my brilliant mind." She laughed softly, still holding him. He turned toward her, but she didn't let go. His left hand touched at her face. She touched his fingertips with her lips.

"I just love you, Rosie. I'll get out of the car here," he told her, twisting her around in the seat and holding her so hard in his hands, she thought she'd break. His mouth closed over hers and she felt as if she were melting. "I'll be back," he said after a long moment that she didn't want to end.

He stepped out of the car, then leaned back in and took her hand. She just looked at him. "When I get back, let's talk about having a baby, huh? Not right away, but—when there's a chance."

He kissed her hand, then slammed the door closed.

She just sat there, staring toward the airplane. She could hear David opening the trunk, getting out his duffel bag and his rifle and the rest of his gear. They'd taken back roads, with Mitch Diamond driving a mile or so ahead to warn them of unforeseen police or PSF roadblocks. He had traveled in battle gear; she wore a pair of faded blue jeans and one of David's sweaters he'd insisted he wouldn't need in Montana, with her field jacket over it.

She saw him out of the corner of her eye as he walked past the left front fender, his duffel bag over his shoulder, the collar of his black field jacket turned up against the wind, his G-3 slung muzzle down diagonally across his back, his hair—it was the most gorgeous hair she'd ever seen in her life, wavy and thick—catching in the wind.

Rose Shepherd licked her lips.

She grabbed at the door handle, twisted it, wrenched it, opened the door.

And she started running as soon as she'd swung her legs out onto the runway surface, chasing him, catching him.

He set down the duffel bag, took her in his arms, kissed her hard on the mouth; he took her breath away.

Then David picked up his bag and started walking toward the plane.

Rose Shepherd stood there, and she realized she was shouting after him. "I want your baby, David Holden! I want your baby!"

Chapter Twenty-Seven

HE'D GIVEN HER the injections from the kit hidden inside the Suburban, then replaced the kit in its secret compartment, putting the spent needles back as well. She'd fought the needle the first time, not resisted the second one.

The marks from the needles would be so infinitesimally small, they would be noticeable only under a microscope, and then only to the eye of a trained medical examiner; hence there was no realistic danger that they would be noticed by Borsoi or the lethally pleasant Ricardo Montenegro.

Now he sat beside the shore, the wind that blew stiff and cold, making little dust devils in the sand, something he noticed only on the most rudimentary level of consciousness.

Geoffrey Kearney stared out to the east. He was so far south of the British Isles that even if somehow he'd been miraculously able to telescope his vision and somehow see over the curvature of the earth, he would have broken his neck twisting it so far to the left.

He remembered the woman who'd been his contact, telling him to liquidate Linda Effingham as a liability; and he remembered how incensed he'd been at just the thought.

What had angered him most was that the contact had been right, of course.

Linda had become the greatest sort of liability imaginable in his business, a zealous amateur with alcohol-induced diarrhea of the mouth, yet someone to whom he was deeply attached, with whom he was hopelessly involved romantically.

The problem was, he loved her more than he loved himself.

"Damn," Kearney said into the anonymous ear of the wind, perhaps overheard by an errant seagull but nothing else.

He loved her.

Which was why he'd given her the B-complex shot and an injection of a mild sedative, rather than a single injection with an empty needle to stop her heart with an embolism.

Rather than stop her heart he would sooner stop his own.

The decision was unprofessional, even irrational, but something that, no matter what lay in store, Kearney knew he would never regret.

Chapter Twenty-Eight

As SMITH THREW the saddle up onto the rail, he heard the barn door creak slightly. He wheeled toward the sound, the wind howling louder as he punched the Beretta 9mm toward the doorway.

Bob Twobears stood there.

"Don't come up on me like that, Bob; I nearly had an unfortunate experience earlier today." Smith holstered the gun and turned back to the saddle, taking the rag from the nail on the wall and starting wipe it down. Araby was already wiped down, eating from her feed bag, fresh straw in her stall.

"They're coming, Matthew."

Smith stopped the rag in midstroke, just listening.

"I know you didn't tell me all of it."

Smith leaned heavily over the saddle, thumbing his Stetson off his forehead. "There's at least one, and if there's one there's more than one. Antiaircraft emplacements. Radar guided and fully set up for relatively sophisticated microwave transmissions. We'll have to take several of the installations at the precise time that we hijack the train, hold the installations, and somehow—probably through threat of death to the personnel there—be able to use them to our advantage. The one flaw in the plan that I described to you —or the most glaring one, at least—was the obvious fact that the Presidential Strike Force wasn't going to let us just take their train down the mountain with all their prisoners and stand there doing nothing. They'll send up helicopter gunships from Fort Makowski and probably scramble the fighter aircraft at Steinmetz Air Force Base. The base, as you told me, has just been turned over to the Presidential Strike Force. It's fair to assume that the PSF has within its ranks jet-qualified pilots or, through coercion or greed, has enough men from the regular Air Force to get up a fighter squadron to destroy us. We have to take those antiaircraft installations and be ready to shoot down anything that comes after us.

"That, Bob, is the part of the plan I left out—mea culpa," Smith concluded.

"We're going to need—"

"Men," Smith interrupted. "More than you've got and this handful of people from Metro." Smith turned away from the saddle and faced Bob Twobears. "You've got the guns. The uniforms you've already said aren't any problem, because you have access to material in the same camouflage pattern and can have the women of the tribe make as many as necessary.

"What this does mean," Smith told Bob Twobears, "is that this stupid rivalry that has persisted between your tribe and some of the other tribes for decades is going to have to end. That's the only way you'll have a sufficient manpower pool to get the job done. You were appointed the war chief by your tribe. And I realize that the political structure of the tribe only gives you authority over matters relevant to tribal defense. This is relevant to tribal defense. You'll have to go to the Council and tell them that all the splinter Patriot groups within the various tribes are going to have to come together for this mission. If you play it alone, you'll lose, Bob."

"You set us up for this," Twobears said, his voice a whisper.

"I set you up for this, yes. This entire area—here through the chimney of Idaho and across much of Washington state—is vital to Makowski's administration. Relations with Canada are at an all-time low because Makowski wants them to be. The FLNA never did anything in Alaska and Alaska has remained almost untouched by everything that's occurred within the lower forty-eight, refugees are flocking there and the Canadian government isn't restricting border crossings by U.S. citizens, which Makowski has specifically asked for.

"If Makowski and his stooge Hobart Townes can dominate this area, Bob," Smith said, approaching Twobears, "they'll be able to close the United States border with Canada. Makowski's afraid Alaska will move to secede from the Union. The more men and women from the lower forty-eight who go there, the more likely that prospect is. If Alaska shuts down the oil pipelines, declares itself an independent state, it would have the wealth—and the talent from the refugee pool—to hold Makowski at bay almost indefinitely and an all-out revolution against Makowski—a general uprising—would be inevitable."

"You're using these prisoners."

"No, I am not. But to do the job right, you'll need manpower. Once that manpower has been assembled you'll be leading the nucleus around which an army can be formed, an army that can keep these border lands free of Makowski's troops, help hold this country together, and eventually become a key piece in the struggle that is taking shape to restore Constitutional government and depose and try Roman Makowski. That is what is at stake here. And the officers whose lives I pray to God we will indeed be able to save will either turn their regular units against Makowski or join your force, giving you professional leadership in the field that Makowski could only envy and never hope to match."

Smith turned away from Bob Twobears and resumed wiping down his saddle.

"Will you help me?"

"Yes."

From a nail on the stable wall Smith took down a dowel rod with an eye hook on both ends. Into one of the hooks he inserted a piece of rag, then inserted the rod, rag end first, into the rear-facing rifle scabbard on the right side of the saddle, drying out the interior.

"What do you want out of this, Smith?"

"Want?"

"You're setting me up to be commanding general of an army. I want to know what—"

"I want to spend the rest of my life with Lilly, to help her raise Wisdom into the man I know he'll be someday. I want to be left alone to do those two things. That is what I want. That is all that I want. As to material things, I own the finest weapons and accessories available anywhere in the world for my purposes, the finest wristwatch, the finest lighter for my cigars, the finest horse. There's a solid roof over the head of the woman I love and food and clothing for her and the boy who's like a son to me. There's nothing you have now or might ever possess in the future that could possibly be of interest to me. Does that answer your question?"

He looked over his left shoulder at Bob Twobears.

Bob Twobears nodded and turned away.

Matthew Smith was finished drying the saddle.

Chapter Twenty-Nine

"I APOLOGIZE FOR the interruption—and for the lack of amenities, Mr. Townes," Hackler began as he sat down again at the opposite end of the long rectangular table. The dinner dishes were being cleared away by one of the American Indian women he'd had brought up from Fort Devon to attend him and the other senior officers. The tablecloth had been liberated from one of Fort Devon's wealthier homes, as had the silver service, the china, and the crystal, as well as the wine, the brandy, and the silver candelabrum that dominated the center of the table.

"Was there a problem, Colonel?"

"When the body of that young Marine was thrown down into the pit, the personnel in both pits started to riot. We hosed them down. They quieted down."

Townes nodded, then said, "I don't want you to think me unnecessarily cruel, Colonel. What we do here is for the good of the nation. Each of those officers you hold there in the pits posed a real threat to President Makowski's vision for the United States. The President is a kind man, and it was his idea that rather than executing these personnel for disloyalty, we might be able to turn them to our cause instead."

Hackler nodded. Kindness? He doubted that.

"A nation cannot be changed so easily, Colonel," Townes went on. "For two centuries the people of this country have pretty well done as they pleased. And because of that countless lives have been lost, opportunities missed. The attack on this nation by various forces from within—like those reactionary lunatics who call themselves 'The Patriots'—only served to bring to a head, bring out into the open, problems that have plagued the United States almost since its inception. We're a country of malcontents. Have you ever thought about that, Hackler?"

Hackler lit a cigarette and said, "No, I guess I never thought about it."

"Well, few people had the vision to see it, and the daring to act. Why did people come to this nation?"

Hackler exhaled smoke, tried to think of what sort of answer Townes wanted to hear, couldn't fathom Townes's point, so just said what he thought. "They were looking for a better life."

"Exactly! But consider the motivation behind that often-heard line. They were discontent with what they had! They were political dissidents, criminals in some cases, economically dispossessed wanderers, the dregs of European society. And they collected here. Obviously, members of those classes better able to govern were drawn here as well. But, try as they might, it was impossible to control the masses as they had to be controlled. Take Canada."

"What?"

"Canada. Can you actually see the Canadian armed forces holding out against a concerted effort by the armed forces of this country? Certainly not. Yet the Canadian government, wholly against President Makowski's wishes, still allows persons with reactionary tendencies to escape these forty-eight states and flee to Alaska. And Alaska! It's become a hotbed of dissent. There's even talk of secession. To quell such an uprising we have to close the borders with Canada." And Hobart Townes, still holding his glass of wine, leaned forward, his tone low, conspiratorial sounding. "This fort and the army you shall build around it with my help will be pivotal to the invasion of Canada that will come. Manitoba, Saskatchewan, Alberta, British Columbia, the Yukon, and the Northwest Territories will be annexed. Then let's see Alaska secede!"

Townes raised the wineglass as if proposing a silent toast. Hackler raised his glass as well.

They drank.

Hackler realized that Hobart Townes, and very likely Roman Makowski with him, was insane. . . .

The four-wheel-drive pickup ground to a loudly crunching stop in the new snow.

Lilly Twobears stood in the open cabin doorway, a shawl pulled tight around her shoulders, Matthew's arm around her waist even tighter.

There was condensation on the passenger-side window and so she couldn't see inside, couldn't see her son, Wisdom. But she knew he was there.

The driver's-side door opened. "Lilly? Want to go down to the truck?"

"Yes, Smith."

They started away from the doorway as Jack Blackfeather shouted to them, "Hello!"

And then the passenger-side door opened. Matthew said, "Go on."

Lilly started to run.

Wisdom—so tall, so straight, so beautiful—stepped down from the truck.

He opened his arms and she let him hold her.

"Welcome back, son," Matthew said from beside her. She leaned her head against Wisdom's chest as he and Matthew clasped hands.

"Mom," he said. "I missed you." And he spoke to Matthew. "I missed you, Smith."

"Your mother and I—well, good to have you home, son."

She would never understand men if she lived a million summers. Matthew and Wisdom wanted to hold each other, wanted to say the same things that were struggling within her heart. But of course, they never would.

So Lilly Twobears let Wisdom hold her as Matthew stood beside her and the two men she loved more than she had ever loved anyone else spoke of simple matters: ". . . a heck of a lot of snow lately. . . . Araby could use a good ride; you'll have to take her out," or, ". . . been studying for the SAT; wish I could find someplace to take it. . . . Was that train really loaded with prisoners like I thought?"

And Lilly Twobears felt a shiver run up her spine.

That was the thing men talked about that frightened her. It wouldn't be long before any excuses about Wisdom being too young to join the Patriots or in some other way fight for his country would no longer hold up.

And then there would be the chance of losing them both.

Her feet were freezing.

Chapter Thirty

THE FIVE MEN from the cold room lay on hospital beds along the far wall of the infirmary.

Their heads were held in a rigid position with wrapped bricks on either side so they constantly looked upward into a light that blinked on and off over and over again mere inches from their faces.

Into each man's left arm ran an IV tube, an array of IV bottles set in multiple racks beside each bed. Aside from the complicated-looking electronic monitoring equipment that beeped and whirred beside each bed, the only indication that the men were alive which Hackler, at least, could discern was that periodically one or another of them would twitch his eyelids, as though caught in some restless and unpleasant dream.

Doctor Masterson, the medical man who had accompanied Hobart Townes to Fort Makowski, was noting something down on a clipboarded chart, deep in subdued conversation with the Fort's own medical officer, Captain Liggett.

Hackler watched Masterson's face.

Masterson didn't look like a movie "mad scientist," certainly not at all like the death camp doctors portrayed in films dealing with the Nazis. He was short, slender, graying, his face slightly wrinkled with what could easily have been smile lines. There was no mad gleam in his eyes, although the thick glasses Masterson wore prevented any un-magnified view of them.

Masterson at last looked up from the chart.

"Colonel Hackler, isn't it?"

"Lieutenant Colonel Hackler, actually, Doctor Master-son."

"Where is Mr. Townes?"

"Resting. He'll come down here later tonight."

"Umm." Masterson nodded. "And, Hackler, what can I do for you, then?"

"I was curious, Doctor Masterson, just what is going on here. I realize this is . . ." He tried searching for a euphe-mism.

"Brainwashing? Don't be afraid to say it. The term itself is a misleading oversimplification, to be sure, but apt to a degree, certainly to the layman's way of thinking. More apropos, I think, however, would be the term *motivational redirection*. I invented it myself." And Masterson smiled.

"Motivational what?" Hackler leaned back against a stool, then perched upon it, alternating his gaze between Masterson and the five men.

"Motivational redirection." Masterson smiled, then, nodding toward the doorway, said, "I want a cigarette. Would you join me?"

"Certainly," Hackler answered, standing, tucking his foraging cap under his left arm and starting to extract his cigarettes and lighter from his uniform blouse. "What's the purpose of the light?"

"The blinking lights?"

Hackler nodded. They reached the doorway leading to the corridor, Hackler allowing the civilian through first. He considered this reconnaissance, so he'd be able to react with the proper enthusiasm at the proper time when Townes arrived.

The corridor was cooler than the infirmary area itself, and unconsciously Hackler hunched his shoulders a little. Masterson seemed oddly unaffected. He lit a cigarette with a match, then searched about, finding a wall-mounted ashtray beside the elevator under a NO SMOKING sign. Hackler lit his cigarette with a disposable lighter.

"The lights," Masterson began again, exhaling, a look of genuine pleasure lighting his face—either the cigarette or the opportunity to explain his procedure the apparent cause—"are to aid in keeping the subject constantly on the edge between sleep and wakefulness—that state in which the mind, as I have found, is most susceptible, in which images are formed most quickly and dreams are most realistic. You may not have noticed the objects beside their heads."

"Bricks or something?"

Masterson laughed. "No. You're thinking of what we used to do years and years ago following cataract surgery. On either side of each subject's head are specially designed units that serve as speakers both in the audible and inaudible range. The light, the sound, and finally the combination of chemicals or drugs that we use, can produce, in the appropriate subject, the motivational redirection I have mentioned."

"Can produce, Doctor?" Hackler walked away, toward the elevator, to extinguish his cigarette.

"Each individual, of course, is slightly different. Oddly, the principal drug that we employ is most effective with persons who have a very strong will. We convince them, basically, of an idea. But the weaker-willed person, less obsessed with his own sense of being right, being correct, may question the idea and therefore not become motivationally redirected. The stronger-willed person, the type who is easily convinced that he is right and often sticks by that conviction in the face of evidence or logic to the contrary, is frequently more susceptible to the ideas we attempt to implant once we convince him these are his own ideas."

"No one more zealous than the convert?" Hackler suggested.

Masterson laughed. "You grasp the idea quite well. Actually, these five men seem to be well suited—ideally suited —to this experiment. If it works, they will become conscientious officers in behalf of Mr. Townes's project."

"And if it doesn't work, Doctor?"

Masterson shrugged his shoulders. "That is Mr. Townes's department and, I suppose, yours."

He rejoined Masterson by the doors leading into the infirmary, not going inside but merely looking in. If the strongest-willed men were the most susceptible to this process, it was indeed truly revolutionary—and it was frightening.

His policy had always been to take the money and run and leave the morality of the thing to the philosophers. Such would have to be his policy this time. The sorts of men he had never desired to emulate but always admired were the most vulnerable. The strong became the weak because of their very strength. He turned his mind off to it, suggesting to Doctor Masterson, "Buy you a cup of coffee?"

"You're on, Colonel."

Chapter Thirty-One

As HE DID every night unless he was physically unable, Matthew Smith removed the fifteen-round magazine from the Beretta 92F, worked the slide back to clear the chamber, visually and tactilely confirming that indeed the chambered round had ejected, then closed the action, depressed the button on the right side of the frame, and flipped the lever on the left side of the frame downward and drew the slide forward and off the frame. He inverted the slide, removed the recoil spring and guide, then slipped out the barrel.

He began to clean the pistol, Wisdom sitting opposite him near the hearth, Lilly humming softly as she put the finishing touches to dessert in the kitchen. It was probably chocolate cake, because that was Wisdom's favorite.

There was a loud crack as one of the logs in the fireplace split.

Wisdom cleared his throat. "So, when, ahh—"

Smith looked up from his gun, the scent of lubricant temporarily obfuscating the more pleasant kitchen smells. "What?"

"I mean, when, ahh—"

"When will somebody try to do something about what's going on at that new fort, right?"

"Yeah."

"Soon. But all great undertakings require planning and preparation."

"Rome wasn't built in a day, right?"

"Something like that. What we're faced with now is a situation more reminiscent of Caesar as he prepared to cross the Rubicon; we're committing ourselves irrevocably. Can you remember what Caesar said? In the original Latin?"

Smith was already reassembling the Beretta.

" 'The die is cast' is it?" Wisdom asked.

"Yes, but Latin, remember?"

"Uhh—*'Alea jacta est!'* "

Smith felt the corners of his mouth turning up into a smile. "Very good, Wisdom."

"Hey, guys—dessert," Lilly called.

Smith looked at Wisdom. "Can't keep your mother waiting." He bumped the magazine up the butt of the pistol, worked the slide with the safety on, the hammer dropping automatically, then removed the magazine, replaced the now chambered round with the one originally chambered, gave the exterior another good wipe-off, and shoved the gun into the leather.

Wisdom was already in the kitchen, leaning up against the counter, working on his cake and ice cream.

Smith went to the sink and turned on the faucet with his elbow. There was a short buzz and water flowed. He'd powered the cabin with a wind-driven electrical generator. He washed the oil and solvent from his hands with dishwashing liquid, rinsed, began to search for a towel, but Lilly gave him one.

"Can I help in this thing to rescue those people from the fort?"

It was an innocent question, a logical question for a boy who was exceedingly smart, tall, strong, and able for his

age, a question Smith had feared since Wisdom had returned.

As he searched for an answer, Lilly said, "If Smith
thinks there's something you can do, well—you know perfectly well he'll ask you to do it."

"That's cool," Wisdom announced.

Smith leaned heavily on the counter and closed his eyes.

Chapter Thirty-Two

MONTENEGRO'S PITTED FACE was partially masked in deep shadow. "So she is sick."

It was a statement, not a question, but Kearney answered it as though it were the latter. Looking up at him, Kearney said, "Yes."

They occupied the deck surrounding the pool behind Borsoi's beach house, Kearney seated at one of the umbrella tables, the umbrella folded away, Borsoi opposite him, Montenegro standing between them and the pool. Kearney sipped at his ginger ale.

Montenegro, as Kearney looked up again, was trying to light a cigarette, but the wind blowing in over the surf a few hundred yards beyond kept extinguishing the disposable lighter. Finally, Kearney stood up, cupping his hands around his solid brass Zippo as he fired it.

"Gracias. So, her being sick bothers you?"

"She's my girl; yeah, bothers me, okay?" Kearney sat down.

"What is she sick from?"

Kearney exhaled, mentally shrugged. The truth was always better than a lie whenever possible. "She drank too much. I get the idea she's been doin' a helluva lot o' drinkin'. Satisfied, man?"

Montenegro rested a hand on Kearney's right shoulder, in almost a fatherly way. "When things go badly with your woman, amigo, the whole world it seems against you. And, the best thing that I have found is to get another one." He clapped Kearney hard on the shoulder and laughed, catching up a spare chair with his right foot, scraping it over to sit down between Kearney and Borsoi.

"She'll be okay, Ricardo. I gotta keep her off the booze, that's all."

"Ha!" Montenegro laughed. "To keep someone from liquor is as hard as to keep someone away from the shit I sell, amigo. Hooked is hooked!"

"She ain't hooked, man," Kearney said, keeping to his punk persona as much as he could. "She drank too much and she isn't used to it, okay? Let it alone, huh?"

"Ricardo is right, in a way," Borsoi said, lighting a cigarette. "But if you're that committed to her, we'll try to help you out. We need your mind wholly on the project at hand. Not on the woman. I'll get some medical people up here that we can trust and they'll work with her."

Kearney shivered, hoped he didn't show it. "Helping" Linda Effingham could mean hypnosis, drug therapy, or just deprivation. Under either condition she might crack, telling what she knew: that instead of a street punk named Thad Borden, he was a British agent. But there was no choice; to reject the offer of help would only draw suspicion. "All right, Dimitri—damned decent of you, man."

"Hey, no problem." Borsoi smiled good-naturedly.

"So that is settled, then." Montenegro nodded. "And now we can get on to other things." All that was missing were the words *more important,* but they hung there, as if actually said.

"Your instruction for your new role begins tomorrow morning," Borsoi began. Kearney lit a cigarette. He wanted to get upstairs to Linda, to see if the sedative had worn off, to see—he worried over her, loved her. Borsoi said, "Most wars, these days, are public-relations battles. They've always been that, of course, only now the public-relations aspects are more obvious.

"In times past," Borsoi continued, as though lecturing before a group of students, "advantage was always taken of mass sentiment in the successful prosecution of a war. The enemy would be portrayed as racially inferior, by nature prone to evil, as thieves, child molesters, rapists, wanton killers. The idea of fighting such an enemy was sold to the public to rally soldiers and civilians alike around the cause célèbre, as it were.

"No one ever fights for the government, even the flag, regardless of the circumstances, the war, or the nations involved. Not even national honor. One fights for concrete values: the preservation of the race, the sanctity of the home, the safety of loved ones, the future of the unborn.

"One of the problems inherent in the FLNA movement from the very outset has been that the FLNA has been seen by the vast majority of Americans as an evil attacking force, destroyers, not saviors. I was aware of that when we began. But then, the time was not right for a popular hero. Now, however, the time is right. The FLNA can become recognized as having fighters for the traditional American values all along, who had been tragically misrepresented in the media and by official government sources.

"We're not nasty, anti-American terrorists. We're for Mom and apple pie and baseball and John Wayne movies. That's what you'll represent, my young friend.

"We needed someone who had the qualifications you possess." Borsoi smiled good-naturedly, stubbing out his cigarette. "We wanted someone who was good looking so he'd appeal to women, but not so good looking as to present anything less than a totally masculine image to men—sort of a Clark Gable type. The women fantasize themselves in his arms, the men fantasize themselves sitting down and having a beer with him and talking baseball, a man who can satisfy a sultan's seraglio, then fight off the sultan's armies with one hand tied behind his back."

Kearney was beginning to feel flattered. To keep in character he asked, "Sera—what?"

Borsoi smiled indulgently. "His harem, the collection of wives."

"Oh."

"We want to present an image the American people will get behind," Borsoi continued. "You are going to be that image. Diction lessons—how to talk. Just the right clothing, everything that is required. We have experts helping us to build the correct image, your image. You will be the man who will stand for the FLNA, and through your positive image, the FLNA will come to be seen as liberators, as Americans fighting in the noble cause of freedom.

"President Makowski's administration is playing into our hands perfectly." He paused, lit another cigarette. "The more repressive his administration becomes, the more the American people will rally to our cause."

He asked a question he had wanted to ask, and one that seemed in character too. "What about these Patriot guys? I thought they billed themselves as bein' out there fightin' for Uncle Sam and all that shit?"

"They do. But soon that will change. For one thing, they're woefully disorganized. With the exception of a handful of leaders, like this pain-in-the-ass David Holden from Metro, they don't have the ability to back up their talk with effective action. Plus, the press has already declared Holden and his ilk outlaws. They won't change. You, on the other hand, will have only a positive image. Since the Patriots are diametrically opposed to the Front for the Liberation of North America and you'll be presented as good personified, Doctor Holden and the rest of the so-called Patriots will only be seen in a more negative light.

"When you bring food to your first orphanage"—Borsoi smiled—"bring blood to your first hospital, shelter some downtrodden family living in a hovel after the Patriots and the Presidential Strike Force have gone after each other's throats in Metro or some other city, you'll have the people begging to follow you."

"What happens then?"

"Makowski is deposed, allowed to leave the United States rather than face public trial and execution, and you, my young friend, will rise on a wave of public sentiment to lead the United States."

"Like the President?"

Borsoi laughed. So did Montenegro. "You can call yourself a god if you want to." Montenegro chuckled.

Borsoi stubbed out his current cigarette. "You'll be the face they see. If you keep that in mind, you'll be rich and well provided for throughout a long and pleasure-filled life. But you will not rule. You understand that?"

"Then you guys, uh—"

"Yes, in a manner of speaking. That's none of your concern, now," Borsoi assured him. "You can reach out, as you Americans say, and grab the brass ring. It's yours. If you're smart enough to content yourself with that— women, money, influence, the finest clothes, the finest cars, world travel, adulation from the masses, babies named after you—you'll have everything. If you attempt to cross us— and I'll warn you now—you will die. Your body will be venerated, your spirit revered, but you will be dead in the ground. Understood?"

Geoffrey Kearney exhaled, wishing he had something stronger than ginger ale in his glass. And he said, "Yeah."

Chapter Thirty-Three

SHE WAS COLD and tightened the sleeping bag around her, burrowing into it.

David should be reaching Montana soon. Rose Shepherd confirmed that by activating the light for the face of her Timex Ironman, beside her pillow. She hoped he'd slept, at least better than she was sleeping.

It was nearly dawn and if she'd slept four hours, she was lucky. And she couldn't get to sleep now.

The cold she felt was very physical, but more than that, mental.

Each time David was away—and inside herself she knew that he would be away from her more and more as the war broadened and his responsibilities increased—it was harder and harder for her to handle it. She was tired of being a freedom fighter, for the first time in her life more interested in being a wife—and a mother.

Her hands were pressing against her abdomen, her fingers splayed across it. And Rose Shepherd wondered what it would be like to carry David's child in her womb. She was healthy. Her gynecologist, an old family friend, had once told her she should settle down and have children. It should be easy for her. Her pelvic measurements, her overall fitness . . . She'd laughed it off then, too involved with her career as a police officer and no man in view she wanted to sleep with, let alone bear a child for.

"Rosie. If your dad were alive he'd be telling you to live a full life."

"I thought you were a groper, not a shrink."

" 'Groper' my ass."

"I thought it was my—"

"Look, Rosie. You're not getting any younger, that's all I'm saying. You modern women. Healthy bodies, healthier than women have ever been, and you don't take advantage of it."

"It depends on what you mean by taking advantage, doesn't it, Doc?"

"You listen to me. Your dad would've wanted grandkids. Go out and make some. I'll take care of you for free."

"Looks to me like I've got probable cause to check this place out for hallucinogenic substances, Doc."

"Talk, talk. You sound more like Jack Webb sometimes than Shepherd's daughter."

She smiled now, remembering she'd glanced past him to the clock on the wall and said, "Ten twenty-seven A.M. My partner Frank and I were working—"

"Fine, Rosie. You laugh. You laugh now." And he leaned forward and kissed her on the forehead as if she were a little girl.

Now she wasn't laughing.

Chapter Thirty-Four

GEOFFREY KEARNEY OPENED his eyes and started to reach for the gun beside him, but realized that what had awakened him was Linda Effingham getting up.

There was a sliver of light through the crack between the bathroom door and the jamb. He heard the sounds of vomiting.

The toilet flushed.

Water ran in the sink.

He swung his legs over the side of the bed, tired, his mouth tasting of too many cigarettes this day.

He heard the sound of gargling, then more water running.

Kearney looked toward the bathroom doorway as the light blinked out. The darkness seemed almost impenetrable for a moment, but gradually he could see her again, now clearly as she walked back across the room, hands clasped against her stomach, looking very frail and too vulnerable in her long, sleeveless white nightgown.

"I'm sorry I woke you up," she said, sitting down on the bed beside him. Her voice sounded strained, tired, weak.

"Don't worry about it."

"I'm sorry for this drinking thing. I had problems years ago when I was in college, but I thought I solved them."

"You'll be all right. I'm sticking with you. And Borsoi's bringing a doctor out here to help you. Borsoi's trying to use me, so this doctor will take good care of you. And, I'll be right here."

"There are two things I want at this very instant."

"What are they?"

"A drink, and for you to hold me. Maybe if you hold me tight enough I won't take a drink."

Kearney turned toward her, folded her into his arms, and held her, her head against his chest.

His lips touched her hair.

She began to sob.

Linda asked, "Love me always?"

"Love you always," Geoffrey Kearney answered. "Always."

He kept holding her while she shivered and cried and held him.

Chapter Thirty-Five

THE DOOR OPENED and Hobart Townes looked terrible and terribly angry. The blow-dried hair was in disarray, the eyes were a little bloodshot, and the face was puffy.

"Do you know what time—"

"I'm sorry to awaken you, Mr. Townes," Eugene Hackler told him. "You said you were interested in seeing some action while you were staying with us at the fort."

"But—"

"I have an informant in the Patriot cell operating out of Kalispell. There's a planeload of Patriots from the Metro area due to land here shortly, to be met by a substantial number of the Kalispell Patriots, including their leader, Bob Twobears."

"Metro?"

"That's just what I'm thinking, sir. You said you foresaw this operation as not only a means of turning military personnel of high rank to support the President's programs, but also a means of drawing out a large Patriot force to attack this fort in order to effect their rescue. What if that means this Professor Holden himself?"

"I'll get dressed at once. Do you have enough manpower? I can get—"

"We'll have to go in stealthily, sir. I already have motorized units standing by. Personnel will be airborne out of here in"—Hackler checked the Rolex watch on his wrist. It was another item liberated from that well-off family in Fort Devon—"in about three minutes. We know where they're landing. We'll have every possible means of escape blocked. And enough men to counter whatever resistance they put up."

"What if the aircraft just takes off again, Colonel?" Townes was starting to sound awake.

"That won't happen, sir. I have snipers going into position to shoot out the tires and we'll have full capabilities of further disabling the aircraft if need be. This could be the big one, and I thought you'd want to be in on the kill, Mr. Director."

"Yes."

Hackler smiled. "I'll send a man for you in five minutes, then, Mr. Townes."

"Five minutes."

Hackler gave the usual Hollywood salute reserved for civilians and did a neat left face and walked away.

He felt like whistling.

Chapter Thirty-Six

SMITH ROLLED OUT of bed and forced himself to stand up. "Smith?"

"Go back to sleep." He'd caught the alarm before it went off, waking up by his own internal alarm instead. "I'm going to take a shower."

"I'll make you some coffee."

"I can—"

"I've tasted your coffee, remember?" And she was getting out of bed.

He had a lot to do. First his calisthenics, then a shave and a shower, then check that everything was as it should be with the wind-powered generator and the storage batteries, then double-check that Lilly and Wisdom had enough wood, although Wisdom was good with an ax. Smith felt better leaving her, knowing that Wisdom was with her.

She patted him on the rear end as she walked past him, and he turned around and looked after her. "What was that?"

"Well, if you don't know, Smith . . ." And she let it hang, laughing a little as she disappeared into the bathroom.

He shook his head, muttering, "Women," then rubbed at his right knee. He was stiff, but the stiffness would go away. . . .

* * *

He'd had half a cup of coffee, a glass of fresh-from-con-
centrate orange juice, and grabbed a bit of toast before
checking the generator and the woodpile. The watch on his
left wrist read a hair after five-thirty. Getting rolling this
early wasn't bad if the day were to be spent hunting, even
fishing. He shook his head as he reentered the cabin. Lilly
was still in her robe and nightgown and he could smell
bacon cooking. Wisdom would be up soon, Smith realized.
The boy's nose for food was uncanny.

"You didn't have to go to all this trouble, Lilly."

"Have some more orange juice."

"Save it for Wisdom," he told her. Frozen orange juice
cost a good deal these days and money was scarce, nearly
as scarce as the orange juice.

"Bob told me he found a source for harder-to-get foods,
that he'll get me some more orange juice."

"Bob is an optimist. I am a realist. Save the orange juice
for Wisdom." Coffee, on the other hand, was abundant
enough, also terribly expensive. He hung up his hat on the
hook by the door and picked up his coffee mug. Lilly had
refilled it and the coffee was hot. Prices for everything were
going up as the value of United States currency kept dropping all over the world. There was a small copper mine
he worked occasionally, small amounts of gold coming
from it as well. The profits from the mine, meager as they
were, but coupled with interest he received from a few
blind accounts he had (wisely) transferred into local banks
provided for their modest needs. Meat could be hunted,
vegetables grown, fish caught. Fruit, ammunition, and
components—coffee—needed to be purchased or, most
times, could be traded for.

Bob Twobears had counseled him once, "You should

take your money out of those banks. If they fail because of the crappy state of the economy, you'll lose it all."

He'd reassured Bob that such would not happen. Those bankers with whom he had placed his funds were aware of the fact that, if they robbed him, he would kill them.

Smith shrugged out of his sheepskin-lined coat and set it over an unused chair, sat down at the breakfast table, and continued drinking his coffee as Lilly took the empty plate that was before him and returned to the stove to fill it.

There was a story told in Chicago, supposedly true, of the early days of the Great Depression and of a gangster who had his personal savings account in an institution that was all but under. With his bodyguards the man had forced his way to the head of the line, producing a gun in one hand and his passbook in the other. That was before openly displaying a firearm was a crime, and it wasn't bank robbery since he'd only taken his own funds.

In a way, Smith almost admired the man's panache.

"What time will Bob be here?"

"In about ten minutes, if he's on time."

"Do you think he'll go along with your idea?"

"He'll go along with it. It's a sensible fallback in the event of a trap."

"I don't like you going; but you know that."

"Yes. I know that," Smith told her. The eggs were sunny-side up and barely cooked, just the way he liked them, the bacon halfway between soft and crisp. "Just hope that our newfound friends from the Metro aren't so civilized that they can't ride a horse if they have to."

"I love you, Matthew Smith. So just don't get killed. And Wisdom loves you too. You're the only real father he's ever had." Lilly looked on the verge of tears.

Smith set down his fork.

He stood up.

Lilly met him halfway, an unbroken egg in each hand. His hands encircled her waist. "You are my wife as surely as if ten thousand holy men recited their finest words for us, Lilly." And Smith kissed her hard on the mouth as he drew her body against him.

Chapter Thirty-Seven

DAVID HOLDEN SLEPT in fits and starts. Each time he at last did fall soundly to sleep the time for changing planes was again upon him.

Their current pilot, from the Patriot group operating out of Cheyenne, Wyoming, and in northern Colorado, was a woman named Myra, no last name supplied.

Holden looked forward past the open curtains and into the cockpit. She was the classic image of the female pilot: leather bomber jacket, a white scarf draped around her neck beneath it, tight-fitting pants and high boots, her long auburn hair caught back at the nape of the neck with a sensible-looking barrette of some sort, the design looking faintly Native American.

Holden shook his head, lit a cigarette, thought about Rosie.

He exhaled, watching the smoke as it ricocheted off the cabin window beside him.

Holden drew the Beretta 92F Compact from the shoulder holster beneath his left armpit. He folded down the small tray table and unloaded the Beretta, then proceeded to check the action. Satisfied, he reloaded it, then proceeded to do the same thing with the full-sized 92F.

He wondered if his behavior was becoming pathological.

He had cleaned each gun twice so far, and emptied and cycled each several times too.

Holden looked at his watch as he stubbed out his cigarette. In about an hour they would be touching down on some rural landing strip. And from the looks of the weather reports they'd gotten on the ground in Cheyenne, lucky to land at all.

"Rosie," he whispered into the steamed-over window.

The H & K 91 was between Smith's knees, chamber empty, muzzle up.

Beside him Bob Twobears drove in such near total silence that once Smith had found himself listening for sounds that the man was still breathing.

There were three vehicles in the convoy, a Ford Bronco, a Chevy Blazer, and, much like Smith's own vehicle, a Chevy Suburban. Smith's was newer, more luxuriously appointed inside, and the best car he'd ever owned in his life. He rarely drove, only when time, distance, or terrain dictated that a horse was out of the question. But he'd spent six months of his life teaching counterterrorist driving and, as a teenager, had stripped and rebuilt his own car and several others.

Five more men with full gear were in the Suburban in which they now drove, three in the center seat, two in the rear seat. Ancillary gear was packed in the space between the rear seat's back and the station-wagon–like rear deck, beside the spare tire.

"Why the hell did you want those horses?" Bob Twobears had asked him before they had entered the car.

Smith told him, "If we don't need them, I'll apologize for all the trouble I put you to. If we do need them . . ." And, as they'd started to enter the Suburban, Smith added, "Only you and Henry Blackdog know about this."

"Henry's with the horses now. You don't trust this operation, do you?"

"You're right," Smith had agreed.

And as he looked at Bob Twobears now, still silent behind the wheel as they moved through the swirling snow with nothing more than their parking lights for illumination, he wondered what Lilly's brother was thinking.

Finally, Smith just looked away.

Chapter Thirty-Eight

HOLDEN TOOK THE copilot's chair across the small console from Myra. "This weather's terrible, professor," she said.

"Are you going to be able to land?" His eyes shifted across the instruments on the copilot's side. The altimeter looked like a barometer in the middle of a storm.

"I've landed in worse. But I figured you should know. And I appreciate the company up here, but when it gets time to set her down, why don't you rejoin Mr. Steel and the others. Safer back there in case we have any problems at touchdown."

"What's that they say about '. . . any landing you can walk away from . . .'?" Holden smiled. "How long you been doing this?"

"Flying or helping the Patriots?"

"Both, I guess," Holden said.

"Flying since I was twelve; my dad ran a charter service up in Alaska. And the Patriots? Pretty much ever since the movement got started. I'm a vet." And she laughed. "Because I'm a woman, the schmucks wouldn't let me fly anything serious." She shook her head and laughed. "But maybe that'll change someday."

"I hope it does," Holden agreed. "I wasn't checking your qualifications, by the way. Just trying to pass the time."

"I understand. How about you? The way you were eyeing the instrument panel there, I bet you can fly."

"A little bit. You learn a little bit about a lot of things in the SEALs, if you have the interest. I wouldn't want to be flying in this, though," he admitted. "You're a lot better than I could ever be."

"Thank you. Daddy trusted me flying one of his planes before he'd even let me behind the wheel of a pickup or anything. Sometimes I have a hard time remembering when I couldn't do this. And, honest to God, I have flown in worse and set her down and walked away. So rest easy. We'll be on the ground in another few minutes."

Holden laughed. "You wouldn't mind rephrasing that, would you?"

She laughed, saying through it, "Get outa here."

Holden started aft, his stomach churning for more reasons than he wanted to count. . . .

The intensity of the wind was beginning to make Matthew Smith wonder if the anticipated aircraft would be able to land at all. But whether it did or didn't, what in his guts he knew was about to happen would still happen, one way or the other.

Ed Greyeagle crouched beside him in the the windbreak made by the Suburban. "Too fuckin' bad Henry couldn't make it!"

Smith looked at him. "As you say," Smith agreed.

"You think these Metro badasses can land in this weather?"

"The prevailing winds make it a little dicey."

And then the wind all but stopped.

Matthew Smith stood up from his crouch.

He pulled the knot open under his chin, lowering the woolen scarf he'd tied over his hat to keep it from blowing away and to protect his ears. He dropped the scarf into the left side pocket of his sheepskin coat. The air almost felt warm, in sudden contrast to the biting wind of an instant before.

And in the stillness, from the east, he heard the sound of aircraft engines.

"Shit!" Greyeagle exclaimed.

" 'Yon gray lines that fret the clouds are messengers of the day.' "

"What?"

"Shakespeare."

Chapter Thirty-Nine

HACKLER SAT BEFORE his command console on the right side of the armored personnel carrier. Battlefield vision-intensification television cameras mounted at strategic locations along the anticipated front, broadcasting to his vehicle by means of satellite, showed clearly that a small Patriot force was in position. Already the pictures were becoming overly bright, and in a matter of minutes he would switch over to conventional video before the hint of gray on the eastern horizon fried the optics in the ultrasensitive units currently on line.

Beside him, standing, leaning over the consoles as if he understood half of what was going on, was Hobart Townes. "You say there's an aircraft coming in?"

"That's right, Mr. Townes. Microphones we have strategically placed—ultrasensitive—have picked up what the computer tells us is a twin-engine aircraft starting an approach."

"Will those microphones pick up the conversation of the rebels out there?"

It was the first time he'd heard the Patriot organization members referred to by that title. "Not sufficiently to be understood, Mr. Townes. We can only tell that they're talking. That much we're able to segregate from background noise."

"Dammit!"

"Yes, sir. But the technology will come someday," Hackler reassured him. He looked up into Townes's face as he spoke. There was a greenish cast to Townes's skin, imparted by the monitor screens in the otherwise gray interior of the APC. "I wish this wind had died down earlier. I can't bring my airborne people in now, because the approach of their aircraft would tip the Patriots—I mean, the 'rebels,' that is."

"Yes. But you have enough personnel on the ground already, right?"

"We have ninety men in position. Every possible avenue of escape from the mesa is covered. And if they fled toward the east, they'd be on foot. Once that aircraft touches down and those Metro people are on the ground—Professor Holden hopefully one of them—my men close in from the north, south, and west. Easy prey. Would you like a cup of coffee, sir?"

"Yes, yes."

Hackler called over his shoulder to his orderly. "Make it two, Corporal."

"Yes, sir."

Hackler signaled the switch from vision intensification to standard video.

Chapter Forty

HOLDEN'S HANDS WERE folded white-knuckle tight over his abdomen as Myra started the Beechcraft's final approach toward the snow-covered mesa below, brilliant yellow sunlight reflecting from the mirrorlike white, his eyes squinted against it. "Rosie," Holden whispered. He didn't want to die, certainly not like this. To die in combat for what he believed in was another thing altogether.

When he'd first become involved with the Patriots, he'd literally had nothing to live for, his wife, Elizabeth, and the children murdered, victims of the Front for the Liberation of North America's terrorist attrocities. But now there was Rosie.

Myra's voice came over the intercom. "There is no cause for alarm, but due to the rugged nature of the terrain below us, you should assume the crash position I explained before takeoff."

Bill Runningdeer, sitting opposite Holden, said, "God help us."

Holden took up the pillow from the seat beside him, checked his seat belt again, and started to lean forward. . . .

Matthew Smith told Ed Greyeagle, "Get everybody ready. The plane's coming down."

"Fuckin' A!" And Greyeagle shot him a thumbs-up.

Smith stared after him as Greyeagle jogged off through the calf-deep snow toward the Suburban, where Bob Twobears and the rest of the men from the Kalispell Patriot Cell were congregated.

The twin-engine Beechcraft was coming in smoothly from the west, having circled the mesa twice following its initial approach from the east. The engine noises were even, almost reassuringly so.

Smith looked to his rifle, chambering the top round off the twenty-round magazine already inserted, a second twenty-round magazine clamped beside it, right side up, ready to be swapped into position. He kept the rifle forward, his thumb beside the selector so he could shift from safe to fire.

There was no indication that his assumption had been correct that a trap was awaiting them, but there was no reason to believe that all was well either.

The presence of the Metro Patriot personnel would be critical to any possible chance of success against Fort Makowski, for the theft of the train, the freeing of the military prisoners there. But he had also used the Metro Patriots as a means of flushing out the traitor he had known for some weeks worked within the Kalispell Patriot Cell. A fine gentleman of his acquaintance, a veteran of World War Two, a career intelligence field-operative, had told him once, "There is no such thing as accident or coincidence; if you operate on that assumption, you'll live longer." Coincidence and accident.

Smith had alerted the Patriot cell that he would be scouting near Widow's Table for an analysis of Fort Makowski. There had been a patrol, which had nearly cost him his life. His left upper arm still bore mute testament to that. Four days before, when he'd helped Twobears and the Patriots during a raid on a two truckloads of weapons and ammunition bound for Fort Makowski, air support for the convoy had arrived unexpectedly and nearly cost them all their lives, five men dead as the result. Abner Groaningbear, a primary financial supporter of the Patriot movement in Montana, had been rendezvousing with several other persons involved in aiding the Patriot movement. As Groaningbear had traveled toward Helena for his meeting, his itinerary known only to the Patriots, his car was intercepted and he was mysteriously assassinated.

The plane was coming in low now, Smith almost thought too low. But he was no pilot.

If he were running the ambush he anticipated, he would wait until the aircraft had landed, perhaps taxied partway back, certainly until the Metro Patriot personnel were disembarked.

He would have men located in fast-moving armored personnel carriers at three of the four cardinal points. To the east the mesa ended abruptly in a sheer drop of over one hundred feet. There was no fast path downward and getting a vehicle down the cliff would have been impossible unless it could fly. The terrain below quickly turned into a narrow gorge, which broadened into a river basin, where, this time of the year, there was only glistening white ice and shoaled frigid pools of water.

Smith looked over his shoulder. Greyeagle was coming back toward him holding the Ruger .223 semiautomatic assault rifle he seemed to prefer over all other firearms. It was a fine weapon.

Bob Twobears and the others were moving rapidly now, running along both sides of the landing area, lighting the flares that would guide the aircraft on its final approach.

As the clouds parted briefly, Smith could see the Beechcraft in better resolution. Its landing gear was coming down.

"God help us," Smith murmured.

Greyeagle came to stand beside him. "They're sure as shit comin', huh?"

"Yes. You seem excited, Ed."

"I've been looking forward to this."

"I'll bet you have." As the aircraft's attitude shifted slightly, Smith could see its landing lights. He looked at Greyeagle. "Would have been a shame to have postponed the landing; you know, have them be unable to come in because of those high winds and have to set a new rendez-vous."

"Damn right, man."

Smith shifted his rifle into his left hand and took a step forward so his back was turned toward Greyeagle. "You know, if these Metro Patriots are as good as they appear to be, we'll have a real chance against Fort Makowski—not a big chance, but a genuine one at least."

Greyeagle said nothing. Smith thought he heard the rattle of a sling.

Smith turned around.

The engine sounds of the aircraft were becoming steadily louder.

The muzzle of Greyeagle's rifle crossed Smith's body plane and stayed there.

"You're so fuckin' smart, Smith."

Smith let himself smile. "Under the circumstances I'll take that as a compliment."

You move a hand toward that holster or for that little hideout in your pants, you're dead meat."

"The commander of Fort Makowski's PSF detachment has us surrounded, correct?"

"Got that, motherfucker."

"Why did you become a traitor, Greyeagle?"

Ed Greyeagle's eyes looked nervous, shifting right and left, apparently waiting for the trap to be sprung.

"Why, Ed?"

"You care, man? Huh! Shit!"

"In a way, I do care. Why?"

"Money. You try bein' a damn Indian and see if money don't sound good to you!"

"Bob, Henry, the rest of them; they're Indians."

"Why the hell should I be loyal to a country that screwed me from day one, man?"

Matthew Smith said, "I suppose it's a question of alternatives. Historically, Native Americans were indeed mistreated as you suggest, but Native Americans fought in both world wars and Korea and Vietnam, and they have a stake in this country. And if things aren't ideal, conditions would be worse under the totalitarian regime Roman Makowski and his minions are seeking to impose upon all Americans. So setting aside such psychological subterfuges, you sold out for money."

"Yeah, that's it, man, whatever the hell you said."

"Are you the only one?"

Greyeagle's face laughed, but the dark eyes, which still darted right and left, didn't.

"Are you?"

"Damn right. That's why they need me. I'm set either way, but if that Holden dude's on this plane, I'm on easy street forever, Smith."

"Or, possibly, under it."

Greyeagle's eyes stopped moving, stared into Smith's own eyes. "What?"

Smith's right hand swept up, the little Beretta .25 already in his hand since the moment Greyeagle had started back, hammer fully cocked, safety off. It had been clumsy holding it. The right first finger of his glove was slit where the finger met the palm, so his bare finger could actuate the trigger and to someone looking at him, it would appear the hand was empty.

He punched the pistol forward and shot Greyeagle in the left eye, stepping out with his left foot, crouching as he dodged away from the muzzle of the rifle, firing a second time, into Greyeagle's wide-open mouth, the rifle discharging into the snow. Smith fired again, then again, into the thorax and into the right eye.

The rifle fired again. Greyeagle's entire body seemed to tremble. He was dead before he fell face down into the snow.

Smith safed the Beretta and dropped it into the outer pocket of his sheepskin coat, turning around.

His trigger finger was numb from the cold.

Bob Twobears stared at him, shouted at him, "What the—"

"Greyeagle was a traitor, Bob. And because of him, we've got more important problems now." Smith changed right-hand gloves as he ran toward the improvised field. . . .

The wheels touched, bounced, touched, bounced, the aircraft lurching violently to port, the wheels touching down again, the rush of frigid air over the wings as the flaps went full down, Holden looking up, through the window beside him, the entire plane seeming to vibrate, the aircraft firmly on the ground now but nowhere near stopping, he realized.

In the gray light he could see flares sputtering along the edge of the field, a high mountain mesa of some sort, larger than Holden had imagined it would be, beyond it the sweeping vista of mountains ranked one after the other, range upon range it seemed, covered in snow that sparkled under the sunlight like sugary icing on a wedding cake.

Men. Vehicles. He saw three vehicles parked at one edge of the field and, as he looked to his left, where Runningdeer was sitting up, through that cabin window caught a fleeting glimpse of two vans, a man standing beside each of them, the vehicles' engines running, exhaust fumes billowing. Gone. Whiteness, nothingness.

Holden looked back through his own window.

Details of the snow-covered ground were becoming clear as the aircraft slowed. "Luther, Bill, everybody." Holden craned his neck, looking aft for faces, popping up almost one at a time from between the seats. "As soon as we stop and Myra gives us the signal, we disembark and move out as planned to secure the field while we board the vehicles. I don't want to rely on just their security. Looks pretty cold outside, so we'd better start suiting up."

Holden took up his liner-fitted black M-65 field jacket from the seat beside him. . . .

Hackler's right hand sweated as he curled his fingers around the microphone stand. "This is Hackler. Commence Operation Snare on my signal." His eyes were riveted to one of the monitors, which gave a full view of the field. The aircraft was at a dead stop. A fuselage door opened.

A figure appeared in the doorway, the distance so great for the camera that it was impossible to discern anything more detailed than a human shape.

"That's him! It's got to be him! Holden. Order your men in now," Townes snapped.

"The aircraft is—"

"Order your men in now, Hackler! That's my order!"

Hackler looked at Townes for an instant, then turned to the microphone and ordered, "Commence Operation Snare. Go. Go!"

"We'll get the bastard," Townes was saying. "We'll get him! Tell your men I want Holden alive!"

Hackler had already done that, but said into the microphone, "Commanders of elements Alpha, Bravo, and Charlie. You are reminded of existing orders that Holden is to be taken alive at all costs. I repeat, at all costs."

Chapter Forty-One

As HOLDEN'S COMBAT-BOOTED feet crunched into the snow at the base of the steps built into the open fuselage door of the Beechcraft, he noticed three things: the biting cold, the sound of vehicles faintly in the distance, and a man in a sheepskin coat with a black cowboy hat pulled low over his eyes running toward the aircraft across the snow.

"Hurry—get to the cars! Hurry!"

Holden swung up the G-3, racking the action.

"There isn't very much time!"

Steel was down the steps, beside him. "Who is that guy?"

"One of the Indians, maybe," Holden volunteered, starting toward the running man.

But Bill Runningdeer, from the height of the steps, said, "He's white, not Indian."

Holden quickened his pace, the man in the black cowboy hat and sheepskin coat shouting, "Time is running out! Come on!" And the man stopped. Separated from him by perhaps a hundred yards, Holden stopped too.

"Who are you?"

"My name is Smith. I set a trap for a traitor named Ed Greyeagle, who betrayed the Patriots to the Presidential Strike Force. Your coming here was something I knew a traitor couldn't resist, Doctor Holden. And now he's dead. Those engine noises you hear are Presidential Strike Force armored personnel carriers closing in from three of the cardinal directions. I suggest that we exit in the fourth direction."

"What's there?"

"A chance."

"I could get aboard the plane."

"Yes. You could do that. You might even be able to take off without getting shot down. Then again, you might not." The man with the black hat was tall, but not extraordinarily so. He leaned forward slightly as he spoke, as if he were pushing his words, Holden felt. The mustache gave Smith's face a dour expression, and there was an impatience about Smith that Holden instantly liked—here was someone who didn't mince words, didn't waste time. "But if you are half the man your press notices proclaim you to be, you could not ignore the plight of the men and women imprisoned at Fort Makowski."

Holden stared at Smith an instant longer. Then Holden shouted to Steel, by the base of the steps. "Get the gear, and get Myra too. She'll never get off the ground. We're abandoning the aircraft."

"Right."

Holden looked back at Smith. "I suggest we hurry."

Chapter Forty-Two

THEY JUMPED INTO a blue Chevrolet Suburban, Smith telling the man who, Holden realized from catching the name, was the leader of the Patriot cell, "Bob, move into the back, I'm driving." And Smith dropped down behind the wheel, telling Holden, "I'd recommend the seat belt."

Holden buckled up as the Suburban started forward, the passenger doors slamming shut. In the passenger-side mirror Holden saw Steel almost lifting the pilot, Myra, bodily into one of the vans. The other vehicles, four more in all, were rolling now, and over the horizon on the farthest westerly edge of the mesa, Holden saw an armored personnel carrier, one of the new ones said to be replete with the most sophisticated electronic gadgetry and heavy weapons. It seemed to hang suspended in air for a minute, then was after them.

"You're driving east," Holden shouted over the slipstream through the open window, his collar up against the cold, but his neck already numbing from it, his right ear buzzing with the wind.

"You're right, there."

"There's a sheer drop to the east. These cars—"

"Will never make it. I know that. Just hope those APCs are on the slow side." The Suburban skidded and bore true east now, Smith's gloved hands locked on the wheel, his black cowboy hat cocked on the back of his head, his jaw and mouth set hard.

There was a rushing sound from behind them and one of the Kalispell Patriots shouted, "Incoming!"

The Suburban swerved in the same instant the shell hit, Holden averting his eyes, cranking up the window against the shower of snow and dirt and debris thrown up by the explosion, his ears pulsing with it.

"What about air?"

Smith shouted back, "The wind dropped only a few minutes before you landed and they wouldn't have risked bringing air support in and alerting us to the trap. We have about"—Smith checked a black-faced Rolex on his left wrist—identical to Holden's own—"six minutes before the helicopters get here if they're using the staging area that's most logical."

"Where the hell are we going to be in six minutes?"

"Not here!" The Suburban's engine roared, another shell impacting mere yards from them as Smith dodged the wheel left, swerved, recovered, and kept heading east.

The ground already looked as though it were dropping off, and Holden knew that it would. He reached into his pocket for the knit watch-cap there, pulled it on, down over his ears. He zipped his coat.

In the sideview, part of it obscured by snow and dirt from the explosions, he could see the other vehicles, coming fast.

"When I stop this car, everyone pile out and run for your lives to the edge of the cliff. There are ropes buried every three feet in the snow. Or at least there should be. Get down them as quickly as you can. It's a hundred feet and if you fall you'll be dead or crippled. Horses are waiting at the base of the cliff. If you've never ridden before, now's a splendid time to embark upon the hobby of a lifetime. Remember the old adage, The best thing for the inside of a man is the outside of a horse. Be ready!"

David Holden looked behind them again. The new APCs were supposed to be capable of exceptional speed for such a vehicle. Observation confirmed rumor. They were closing fast.

"Where to after the horses?" Holden asked Smith.

"There's a gorge, and once we're through it we cross a river. Tricky footing for the horses, but once that's crossed there is a series of overhangs leading into some large caves. One of those caves is high enough for a man to ride through, and it opens on the other end into a wooded area. Even this time of year the overhead coverage will be satisfactory to evade aerial observation, and there's a handful of small streams offshooting from the river. Icy in the extreme, sufficiently so to mask thermal prints if an observation aircraft were utilizing more sophisticated technology."

"All we have to do is make it there," Holden said.

The Suburban and the other vehicles slightly behind it were fast approaching where the mesa ended abruptly in the cliff face, Holden seeing little but gray, snow-laden sky now. Snow was blowing up in little cyclonic funnels and huge waves of snow were blowing up to the north. He gathered the winds were returning.

The Suburban skidded to a stop, slaloming another dozen or so yards, Smith grabbing up his rifle from between the seats and shouting, "Let's move!"

Holden was out the door, running forward, slinging his G-3 across his back, the wind gusting now, stingingly cold. He pulled his knit cap lower over his ears and neck.

Holden and Smith reached the edge at the same time, Smith saying to Holden, "Get your men down. We'll hold up here. Then cover our descent."

"Right."

Already, ropes were being pulled up out of the snow, great clouds of powder rising, caught up in the wind.

The other vehicles were all stopped now, men running from them toward the edge, Myra between Steel and Bill Runningdeer, Runningdeer's Uzi submachine gun in his right hand. Holden began tying on.

There was a whooshing sound and Holden looked up, another round fired from the lead of the three APCs so far visible on the mesa, the shell exploding about twenty yards from one of the vans. And Holden realized that their marksmanship was not phenomenally poor. They were under orders to get him alive.

"Smith. You and the rest of your people get over the side and wait for us. They want me alive. As long as they see me, they'll keep missing with those guns on the APCs."

Smith looked at him for an instant, then nodded, saying, "Makes good sense. Good luck." Holden handed Smith his rope.

"Take care of her, huh?" Steel shouted to the man called Twobears, shoving Myra toward him none too gently.

"If I don't freeze to death!" Myra shrieked.

Holden said to Steel, "Back to the Suburban, you and me and Runningdeer. Come on!" Holden broke into a dead run, toward the car, another round firing, impacting one of the vans, a fireball, black and orange and yellow, rising out of the whiteness of the snow, beginning to dissipate almost immediately, in the strong wind, into a trailing finger of flame.

When Holden reached the Suburban, he threw down his backpack. "Luther. Bill. Make it plenty evident we're behind the car. If I'm right, they'll angle toward us, but they'll intentionally miss hitting us."

"And if you're wrong, David?" Runningdeer laughed.

"Well . . ." Holden grinned, never finishing the response.

"They'll be exiting those vehicles and try to close with us on foot, if you are right," Steel noted, checking his G-3's magazine seating.

"Then we go into business," Holden told the ex–FBI man.

Holden looked back toward the edge some fifty yards away. Smith and Twobears were still visible, but most of the others were either down over the side or getting ready to make the descent.

"I ever tell you I hate rappeling?" Steel volunteered.

"Really? Gosh, I love it." Holden grinned, his cheeks numbing with the cold.

As he looked back again, Smith was tying some sort of muffler over his cowboy hat and ears, knotting it under his chin. Smith shot them a wave and, in almost perfect unison with Twobears, started over the side and was gone.

"APC slowing, stopping," Runningdeer announced. "Side door opening. Bingo! People to shoot at!"

Holden turned away from the now evacuated cliff edge and brought the G-3 to his shoulder. Another advantage of the G-3 over the M-16 was its reach, the 7.62mm NATO round it fired considerably superior in terminal effectiveness at greater distances to the 5.56mm round in the M-16's the PSF personnel were using.

Runningdeer and Steel's G-3's were shouldered as well. "Hey, Boss," Runningdeer said.

Holden looked at Steel, Steel sighting over his weapon. "What, Bill?"

"If we get killed doing this, does that mean all our federal benefits package is canceled?"

Steel's body shook with laughter. "Shut up, dammit!"

Holden settled on a white snow-smocked target, the

G-3's selector on semi. He fired once, then again, hitting the Presidential Strike Force trooper twice, the body rocking back and down.

And then the gunfire started, the PSF personnel returning fire on full auto, bullets glancing off the bodywork of the Suburban, glass shattering, Steel and Runningdeer firing short automatic bursts, PSF personnel going down.

"How long do we stay here, David?" Runningdeer shouted.

"About another sixty seconds. Then the three of us break for the ropes. You go over the lip first and hang there with that Uzi of yours, cover Luther and cover me. Then, once we're all on the ropes, we drop. Got it?"

"Got it. Tell me when."

Steel shouted, "Second APC opening up. Trying to outflank us. Yeah. The men are taking shelter behind it."

"It'll advance on us in another few seconds," Holden said, firing a burst, taking out at least one more of the PSF troopers.

The Presidential Strike Force personnel were firing on full auto, many of them from the hip, burning through ammunition, making more noise than anything else.

Holden glanced at his Rolex as he changed to the second twenty-round magazine. "We hit the ropes!"

Holden shouldered the G-3 again, firing a short burst, then broke into a dead run for the cliff's edge. At the limits of his peripheral vision he saw Steel and Runningdeeer doing the same.

Runningdeer made it to the ropes first, starting to tie on as Holden turned and fired another burst from the shoulder, killing another of the PSF men, Steel firing as well. Holden fired again, taking out another man, the others starting to fall back toward the second APC, the vehicle advancing on them slowly.

The third APC, no men out of it yet, was advancing from the opposite side of the mesa. A bullhorn sounded. "Surrender, Doctor Holden, and you will not be killed. Surrender! Lay down your weapons."

Holden fired toward the sound of the bullhorn.

Runningdeer shouted, "Come on, guys!"

Holden safed the nearly empty G-3, pushed it behind his back, and grabbed for a rope. Steel was still firing, Holden shouting to him, "Luther! Now! Move it!"

Steel joined him at the edge of the cliff, Runningdeer hanging below, firing his Uzi over the edge, toward the few remaining PSF personnel who had not taken shelter behind one of the APCs.

Holden tied on, moved to the edge, checked the Southwind Sanctions SAS holster with the Desert Eagle—it was secure—and jumped, feeling the pressure from below as someone belayed him.

Holden fed out rope, descending with as much control as he could, given the primitive method, his feet slamming into the rock face, then kicking away and out and down, stopping his descent, his ordinary winter gloves taking the rope burn, his hands warming from it inside them. Steel jumped out, past Holden. Runningdeer seemed born to the ropes, making a perfectly controlled descent.

Holden kicked out again, skidded downward, locked. As he looked up, he could see faces peering over the edge of the cliff. Someone might cut a rope or start shooting. He locked his left hand on the rope, his feet flat against the rock wall, his right hand reaching for the Desert Eagle .44. He stabbed the pistol upward, thumbing the hammer back, with no thought of hitting anything, but firing anyway.

A clod of snow dislodged, more snow exploding as the 180-grain bullet struck into the rocks, the PSF personnel tucking back.

Holden safed the Desert Eagle, punched it blindly into the holster at his thigh and closed the safety strap, then kicked out. His gloves might burn, but he'd reach the bottom faster.

He let himself down the last thirty feet, smoke rising from the palms of his gloves, his hands feeling the heat.

As he hit the bottom, Steel hit as well, Holden absorbing the shock with his knees, dropping to a crouch, thrusting his gloved hands into the snow. Gunfire came from all around him as he looked up from his crouch, some of the men, Smith among them, already on horseback, others mounting up, some of the mounted men firing assault rifles and old lever actions toward the summit.

Holden pulled the zipper down on his jacket, extracted the Defender knife from the shoulder rig, and hacked through the rope. He looked at the palms of his gloves, the leather gone, the wool glove liner beneath frayed.

As he sheathed the knife, Smith shouted down to him. "Here!"

Holden grabbed the reins Smith thrust toward him. They belonged to a gray horse with black mane and tail, a western stock saddle on its back.

Holden reached for the saddle horn, his left foot into the stirrup, hauling himself up, half falling into the saddle, but aboard. "You lead the way, Smith!"

"My pleasure!" And Smith shouted to the riders around them, "We're moving! Let's ride!"

Holden's horse started forward, Holden fisting the saddle horn with his left hand, the reins in his right as he slapped his heels against the animal's sides.

He was in the middle of the pack now, walled in by human and animal flesh, grim-faced men, most of them Indians, clinging to their animals, the animals' eyes wide with fear or excitement or both, a literal thunder deafeningly loud from all sides of him. Clods of dirt and snow rained around him, pummeling his legs and back and arms and sides, his eyes squinted against them as he leaned forward in the saddle, the gray's mane whipping across his face in the slipstream.

And, from above and behind them, the roar of gunfire over the cacophony of hoofbeats.

Chapter Forty-Three

THE GORGE WAS so narrow, it was necessary for them to ride in single file, and then the V of rock beneath the horses' hooves was even narrower still.

And then the gorge was gone, widening 'impossibly quickly into a canyon, the rivulet of water that coursed along the floor of the gorge funneling into a huge, ice-slicked pool. And Holden realized they had reached the river.

Smith reined in. "Across the river. Three men stay back. Bob, lead them."

"I'll stay back with you," Holden shouted.

"Yo," Runningdeer called out.

"Me too," Steel added.

Bob Twobears shouted to the rest of the men, "Follow me!" And he urged his horse ahead, off the rock shelf and into the water, the animal seeming to founder for a moment, catching itself then, charging on, the others surrounding Twobears and his mount in a ragged wedge, the ice-glistening water rising in sun-shimmering waves around them.

Holden looked up. The clouds were parting overhead, the wind subsiding against his already numbed face. Smith said, "We have substantial difficulties in store, I'd suspect. Their helicopters won't be grounded anymore."

Holden just looked at Smith, nodded, swung his rifle

forward, extracted the magazine clamped to the fully emptied one, stuffed them into the side pocket of his field jacket, and reached to the still unfamiliar-seeming pouch at his belt, extracted a single twenty, and rammed it up the H & K's well.

Runningdeer's horse pawed the ice-slicked rock, nearly lost both its balance and its rider, but Runningdeer held on.

Smith looked skyward. "Hear anything?" And he looked at Runningdeer.

"No."

"Interesting. A fully urbanized American Indian with as poor hearing as the average white man. I hear. Listen harder. From the west—make that southwest."

Holden strained to hear over the clacking sounds of his own animal's hooves.

And he heard it too, now, Runningdeer saying, "Helicopters. A lot of 'em."

"There you go!" Smith laughed, then reined back on his horse. "I shouldn't have let the three of you stay with me. Because we have a hard ride ahead of us the next few minutes. We go off straight downstream through the center of the cut. It'll be slippery, dangerous, but we have to lead off the helicopters."

"You heard them, then?" Runningdeer said, sounding amazed.

"No. I anticipated them, sir. Gentlemen!" And Smith, his rifle in his right hand, thwacked the horse's rump with the barrel and the animal vaulted into the riverbed.

Holden shook his head, shouting, "Come on!" And he prodded the gray into the water. The animal jumped, a wave of water welling up on either side, Holden soaked to the skin from the navel down as the waves crashed over his lower body. Smith's animal charged ahead, down the center of the shallow, ice-splotched riverbed, Holden's animal right behind, Holden holding to the saddle horn more tightly with each almost missed step.

The noise of the gunships was getting louder, the air seeming to vibrate with it.

Holden shouted to the animal, "Gyaagh!" His heels hammered against its sides and the horse's pace quickened, Holden nearly abreast of Smith and the water-gleaming black Smith rode.

And Holden looked back.

Four military helicopters, Apaches, swarmed over the river behind them.

Holden called to Smith, "We'll never make it this way."

"Suggestions?"

"Dismount and open up on them. Just two of us. The other two take the horses on ahead to someplace where we can rendezvous if we make it out."

"Agreed. Around that bend!" Smith's horse leapt ahead, Holden holding his mount back, shouting to Steel and Runningdeer behind him, "Around that bend—then Smith and I'll dismount and open fire on those choppers. You take the horses ahead and find a good spot to wait for us."

"Right!" Runningdeer shouted, but Steel's face, the jaw already set as he clung to his animal, took on a cast still grimmer looking.

Holden kicked into his animal and the horse started ahead again, in the wake of Smith's.

The bend came up quickly, a reentrant from the far bank, studded with trees and rimmed with massive boulders, thrusting into the the center of the riverbed itself, the water twisting around it. In the spring there would be rapids here, Holden thought.

He kept riding, Smith disappeared behind the peninsula now. And as Holden crossed its leading edge, Smith called to him, "Over here!"

Holden reined back, the animal wheeling a few degrees left, nearly falling. Holden swung down out of the saddle, holding the horse's reins with both hands, Holden's legs knee deep in the frigid river-water. Passing him, Steel's mount slowed, reared slightly, Steel holding the animal in control by sheer physical strength, it seemed. Holden passed Steel up the reins. "Don't wait too long."

Steel nodded. "If you get killed, remember something, Rosie will probably kill me when I tell her. I wouldn't want that to happen."

"I'll keep it in mind," and Holden slapped the gray's rump, Steel riding off, Runningdeer joining him, holding the reins of Smith's big black.

"Over here!"

Holden looked around to see Smith clambering up into the rocks at the edge of the peninsula, up out of the water. Holden started to run, realized the footing was slick and treacherous, slowed his pace a little, then looked back. The gunships were closing.

Holden reached the rocks, then started to climb up, seeing Smith already wedged into a one-man rock fortress, shouldering an H & K 91, the once civilian legal semiautomatic-only version of the G-3.

Whoever this Smith was, he had good taste, Holden reflected, reaching the higher rocks, dropping down into a similar nest of boulders about a dozen yards from Smith. "When they fly overhead, we shoot for the tail rotors, right?" Holden called.

"I'm beginning to like you, Professor Holden. And more and more I'm becoming convinced I made the right decision in requesting your assistance in the matter of Fort Makowski."

"The military prisoners, yes."

"That interesting-looking sidearm on your right thigh—a Desert Eagle, of course, but the caliber?"

"Forty-four Magnum."

"Ah—you'll have to let me try it, if you will. I've only fired the three fifty-seven, and that was some time ago."

"Feels like a forty-five, recoil-wise," Holden told him. The gunships were nearly directly overhead, Holden thumbing the selector to auto, readying himself.

Smith held his rifle in something like a shotgunner's ready stance, a quick snap to the shoulder implicit in the way he held his body.

David Holden sighted on the nearest of the machines, then left it, moving to the one farthest over the river bed, leading it slightly as it passed.

"Ever hunted the big Canadians?" Smith asked suddenly.

Without looking at him Holden answered, "No—a little pheasant a couple of times, and that's it with birds."

"I was about to remark that, although bringing one of these down will be more difficult, the situations are a bit similar. If we get all four down and any of the crew survive, we should see that they don't continue to."

"Yes."

"Whenever you're ready," Smith said. And Smith's rifle cracked, Holden's firing in the next instant, both of them hitting the tail section of the helicopter farthest out over the river, but missing the rotor itself. Then Holden fired again, then again, then again, the last burst chewing into the blades and the green gunship instantly started to spin.

Holden swung left, but as he did, the tail section of the already injured craft slammed into the passenger compartment of the second gunship, the second gunship exploding in midair, the first gunship aflame, spinning out of control.

As Holden swung farther left, across the sights of the

G-3 he could see one of the third chopper's rotor blades shearing away, the entire tail rotor spinning off, the gunship starting to screw on its main axis.

As Holden swung left again, the fourth chopper was already hit, smoke trailing from a fuel line. Holden fired toward the tail rotor, missed, the gunship veering away, climbing, narrowly missing the third helicopter as it impacted the second and both exploded, crashing downward into the riverbed.

Holden drew back, the wave of heat washing over him, catching his breath.

He saw Smith, running from cover, his rifle hanging at his side on its sling, a Beretta 92F in Smith's right hand. The last Apache swung around, toward them, machine-gun fire tearing across the water, homing in toward them.

The first helicopter exploded as it impacted the surface of the river and Smith fell back, to one knee, the pistol in his right hand at the full extension of his arm. Smith fired, then fired again and again.

He was aiming for the main rotor, had to be.

Holden moved, pushing himself up from his rock nest, tripping, catching himself, running out along the spit to get a different angle on the gunship.

Machine-gun fire tore across the rocks.

Smith knelt there, firing as if he were in some sort of marksmanship competition.

As Holden brought his rifle to the shoulder and triggered a burst for the tail rotor, the gunship's main rotor suddenly hesitated, stalled.

The gunship fell.

Holden dived away as the blast came. . . .

Smith, the muffler gone and the cowboy hat cocked up from his forehead, sat by the edge of the rocks, feet dangling over the rushing water, a fresh magazine going up the well of the Beretta pistol.

David Holden moved toward him. "Should be a good walk to where Steel and Runningdeer are waiting," Holden said, swapping magazines for the G-3.

"You're a good man, Doctor."

"So are you, Mr. Smith."

"You're too kind."

"How the hell did you nail that main rotor?" Holden grinned.

"All skill"—and Smith looked up at Holden over his shoulder, a smile lighting his face.

"Indeed." David Holden nodded.

"On the way back—you and any two of your friends will be staying with us at our cabin, and Lilly's a wonderful cook, by the way, among her many virtues—we can survey Fort Makowski. We need to hit the fort as soon as we have the manpower assembled. That shouldn't be too long."

"No more traitors to flush out?"

"Not of which I am aware, Doctor Holden."

"Just a mission rational men might term suicidal? That's all?"

"That is all, indeed. But rather than dwell on that, as we rejoin your companions, let me tell you about Lilly and this marvelous rabbit ragout of hers. And by the way, Bob Twobears's wife is nowhere near Lilly's caliber in the kitchen. So you might care to keep the two men you're closest with with you at our cabin. What she does with rabbit is beyond description, really, but I'll try to capture it for you."

David Holden lit a cigarette. Smith fired a cigar.

They began to climb up from the rocks and toward the trees. From there it would be a hike along the shore until the reunion with Steel and Runningdeer. After that—David Holden decided to concentrate on the rabbit stew for the time being. "Let me guess at the recipe. First you shoot a rabbit or two."

Epilogue

LINDA EFFINGHAM WAS absent from lunch and Geoffrey Kearney, after asking some of the other women who were seemingly always around for Borsoi and Montenegro if they had seen her, set off along the beach. A redhead named Lina, rather pretty looking but not the sort of woman who impressed someone with intellectual capacity, had told him, "She went out. That way."

That way was south.

When Kearney saw the dark shape in the surf, he stopped.

And then he bolted toward the shape. "Linda! Linda!"

The shape never moved, except as the surf jostled it slightly farther up the beach.

Geoffrey Kearney fell to his knees in the foam, the body lying there.

He rolled the body over in his hands, already knowing. Her beautiful eyes stared into the cold sun.

"Linda—"

He lowered his head against his chest and tried to breathe, but something wasn't working right and he couldn't because his throat was closed.

He took Linda Effingham up in his arms and hugged her to him, vomit rising in his throat.

She was drowned. He turned his face away and retched.

He would never hear her voice or see her smile or feel her touch again except in memory.

Linda wasn't the sort for suicide.

And she swam beautifully.

He held her body against him, his lips pressing against the cold dampness where once there was warmth—her cheek—

Geoffrey Kearney whispered.

The voice wasn't one he recognized, but he knew it was his.

His words were the only expression of love and grief and eternal sorrow he could muster, now. "You're a walking dead man, Borsoi. A walking—"

And Geoffrey Kearney wept, holding Linda Effingham tightly, so tightly.